LENN WOOLSTON

SUCH GOOD BONES

LENN WOOLSTON

PERCY'S HEART PRESS

Percy's Heart Press www.percysheartpress.com

Book Layout

Edited by Carla Lewis, Jess Moore

Cover Art and Design © 2024 Adina Chiles

Interior Formatting by Book Savvy Services

Credit to: Keats, John. "This Living Hand", *The Poetical works and Other Writings of John Keats, Volume III—Prose*, 1889

Content Warning; Depictions of Suicide.

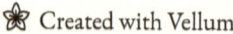 Created with Vellum

For readers who love weird and twisted. Welcome Home.

This living hand, now warm and capable
Of earnest grasping, would, if it were cold
And in the icy silence of the tomb,
So haunt thy days and chill thy dreaming
*   nights*
That thou would wish thine own heart dry of
*   blood*
So in my veins red life might stream again,
And thou be conscience-calm'd—see here it is—
I hold it towards you.

John Keats
"This Living Hand"

Contents

One

C hloe couldn't wait to continue the massacre. She wanted to rip its mouth open and peel back each layer until it was stripped bare. After all, a house was not a house without a good set of bones.

Driving up the spindly two-lane highway, Chloe's mind spun as she eagerly looked out the passenger side window of their crossover SUV. After driving a little over four hours toward the Sierra Nevada, the sky brightened to blue, instead of the depressing gray Bay Area smog disguising itself as a marine layer. Giant pine trees replaced skyscrapers and congested traffic. Chloe rolled her window down and inhaled. Petrichor laced the mountain air. She relished the earthy scent with another long inhale as she noticed pools of water collecting in the rich, copper soil. They passed a large, carved wooden sign with bold letters stating, "Hallowed Pines, Population 327." Thick vines of poison oak wrapped around the sign's wooden posts, their familiar shade pricking her mind. Chloe sat up in her seat.

The swatches.

"I forgot to show you," Chloe said, shuffling around in her messenger bag. She pulled out a three-ring binder full of color tabs and fabric samples. "I found *the* perfect wallpaper for the living room. It's a beautiful woodland baroque-style design that will go well with the wainscotting. I got confirmation that it was delivered to the house last week, so we can put it up right away. Here, take a quick look."

Philip peeled his gaze off the road. "Wow, that's gorgeous. You really have a great eye for design, babe."

Chloe smoothed the patch of wallpaper in her binder. "The building has been vacant for so long. I'm sure it will welcome a new set of skin. The living room has enough space for a bold pattern. I don't think we'll have any problem reaching a perfect kill point."

Philip sighed. "You always have to be so morbid, don't you?"

"Hey, that's what they call it in the interior design world." Chloe closed her home décor binder and turned to face him. "The kill point is where the first and final pieces of wallpaper meet."

"Ah, yes," he replied with a nod. "The 'new skin,' right?"

She nudged his arm with her elbow. "It adds some personality to the home. You know, in some cultures, people talk to their houses. Some even give it a name."

"I see." Philip scratched the bridge of his nose underneath his wire-framed glasses before flipping up the sun visor. "So, it turns out I'm not the only practicing physician after all, what with you tending to buildings like I do to patients."

Chloe smirked as she adjusted her seatbelt. "Physician? No, my four years of design school don't compare with your hard work, Dr. Blackwell." She swallowed the sour tang of her parents' words. "If only my parents would be proud that I'm finally putting my degree to use."

Philip reached over, sliding his hand underneath hers. Intertwining their fingers, he lifted her hand to his lips. "You always make me proud," he whispered and kissed her skin.

Proud. A word so foreign to Chloe. She considered her parents to be bilingual—fluent in sarcasm and criticism. *Focus on math instead of art, dear,* they'd told her in elementary school. *What good is an interior design degree in today's market,* her father questioned her at her college graduation dinner. *He's too mature for you,* they said after meeting Philip for the first time. *His on-call hospital shifts will be the death of your marriage,* her mother warned when Chloe shared the news of their engagement. Chloe was convinced her parents drank her tears like a fine wine, savoring every drop of sadness. She had given up trying to figure them out a long time ago, but spending twenty-four years in her parents' household had taught her two things: Pain is inevitable and survival is beauty.

Now, with her hand cradled in her fiancé's, Chloe grinned and thought, *Fuck them and what they think of me. They aren't invited to the wedding anyway.*

"I love you," Chloe said, giving Philip's hand a gentle squeeze.

"I love you too." Philip returned the action, then let go of her hand. He settled his grip back on the steering wheel. "Hey, can you crack open a bottle of water for me? I swear, this mountain air always makes my allergies flare up."

Chloe reached down and twisted the cap off a water bottle. "What? You already miss the Bay Area pollution? I thought the mountain air was better for your lungs."

"You know what I mean," Philip said as he playfully swiped the bottle from Chloe's grasp.

Chloe watched as he tilted his head back, appreciating him. Philip was the type of person who seemed to be born in the wrong era. Sure, he was twelve years older than her, but Chloe didn't mind the age gap. She admired his chiseled jawline under his dark brown five o'clock shadow. She enjoyed the way he brushed his wavy brown hair back, exposing his receding hairline. He was romantic, preferred phone conversations instead of text messages, enjoyed home-cooked meals over racking up Uber Eats rewards, and above all else, he was always willing to help others.

A gentle warmth bloomed inside her as she recalled meeting Philip for the first time. After Chloe had sliced her hand on a broken wine glass in a crowded San Francisco bar, Philip ushered her safely to his apartment less than a block away to tend to her wound so she could avoid a hefty emergency room bill. Maybe it wasn't love at first sight, but it was love at first stitch and that was enough for her.

Chloe smoothed the hem of her sweater. "Do you think your parents are going to be able to stop by the house while we're here? I'd love for them to see all the work we've done on the place."

"Shoot, I forgot to tell you," Philip replied shaking his head. "They took a last-minute trip to South Carolina to help a church family in expediting their tiny home operation before the summer heat starts."

"South Carolina?" Chloe asked, twirling a chunk of her hair around her finger. "Why so far?"

"It's part of some ministry," he explained. "They've been helping installing tiny homes, creating a positive community for the homeless. I guess there are about twenty families ready to move in, so a member of the east-coast chapter congregation asked for volunteers. But don't worry, they'll be back in time for the wedding next month."

"Oh, that's so kind of them," Chloe said with a lopsided smile. She had only met Philip's parents twice before, and she couldn't gauge whether his parents considered her worthy enough to become part of the family. Philip admitted he prayed every now and then, but he left most of his religious practices and beliefs behind after moving to the city for college. The closest Chloe ever came to being considered religious was when she cried out to God while in bed with Philip. "You don't think they're still upset that we're converting your family's old church into a house?"

"What?" Philip glanced at her and then steadied his eyes on the road. "Of course not. They are happy someone in the family is doing something with it. My younger brother is too busy traveling in New Zealand, and my older sister is in Tennessee. So, really, it's kind of fallen on my shoulders since I'm the only child still in California. But after they see what we do, how *you're* going to work your incredible magic on the inside, I have no doubt all of them will be proud of us."

Proud. That word again. Chloe twisted in her seat as butterflies took flight in her stomach. "And they liked your idea of us putting it on the market after the wedding, right?"

Philip snapped his lips closed. He cleared his throat, reaching for his drink in the cup holder.

"Babe"—Chloe watched him rush the water bottle to his mouth—"please tell me you told them we aren't moving out of the city."

Philip swallowed hard, choking on the last sip. "I—I will."

"Philip," Chloe cursed and turned off the radio. "You

were supposed to tell them our plan. Wait, you're not having second thoughts, are you?"

"No," Philip said, locking eyes with her. "Of course not. Our lives are in the Bay Area. They get that. I just haven't fully told them we intend to sell this place so we can buy a home in the city. It's not going to be easy for them to say goodbye to the property that's been in my family's name for four generations."

Chloe placed her hands in her lap as her heart sank. Not only did she worry about what Philip's parents were going to say when they heard the news, but she also worried about what kind of wedge this was going to drive into their relationship. Announcing their quick engagement had been a shock, nothing a little time couldn't heal. But this? This had the potential to be as catastrophic as an earthquake tearing the Bay Bridge in two.

Chloe parted her lips, an apology forming on her tongue. But a dark figure flashed in her peripheral vision.

Time slowed as she peeled her gaze from Philip. Two black eyes locked onto hers. Chloe's heartbeat pounded against her eardrums. Adrenaline shot through her veins, piercing every inch of her skin.

"Philip!" she shouted and pointed to the windshield.

He turned his attention back to the road. The brakes squealed as Philip twisted the steering wheel to the left. The deer ran across the roadway, becoming a blur of brown. Their tires swerved over the double yellow line as Philip tried to slow the car. A fawn leaped over the hillside. Its legs scrambled against the asphalt as it tried to catch up to its mother across the road. Chloe screamed as she gripped the door handle, bracing herself.

Metal crunched upon impact. The left side of the car

lurched up and forward as the tires rolled over something large. A loud pop erupted.

"Shit," Philip said with a huff. "Oh my god, Chloe. Are you okay?"

She slowly opened her eyes. Dust swirled in the air, curling around the raised corner of the SUV hood. She exhaled in relief at seeing the dashboard still intact.

Her arms burned with the electricity of adrenaline. Her lower lip trembled. She unlocked her death grip on the handle. A throbbing pain pulsed at her hairline. She wiped her hair back, examining her fingertips. Not a drop of blood appeared on her skin. Relief that they hadn't hit the full-grown deer flooded through her, but *oh god*, the baby.

"I'm okay," she responded through a shaky breath.

"Good," Philip murmured. He pried his hands from the steering wheel and turned the ignition. The idling engine stopped. Reaching over, he smoothed her hair back. His fingers traced along the back of her neck as he gently pressed into her skin, examining her.

Chloe's chest tightened. "Oh god, the deer." She turned toward Philip in her seat. Tears pooled against her eyelids. "Is it..."

"Dead." Philip swallowed hard. "At least I hope it is."

Chloe dabbed a sore spot forming on her forehead. Glancing down, she noticed the splatter of colors across her lap. The accident had caused her décor binder to spew paint swatches, magazine clippings, and fabric samples everywhere. But she was still alive.

"What should we do?"

Philip sucked in a breath as he pulled back her hair from her face. His fingers brushed against her skin as his eyes searched her face. "No sign of bleeding. Pupils are equal, round, and reactive. Neck is—"

"Hey," Chloe said, pulling away from his touch. "I'm fine. No need to dictate a full examination."

"It's what I do," he admitted. "I need to know you're okay."

A car honked twice from behind them, stealing their attention. Chloe checked the passenger side mirror. An over-sized red truck pulled off the road and parked behind their SUV.

"Thank the Lord," Philip murmured.

Chloe followed Philip as they both carefully got out of their vehicle. The diesel engine rattled the air before the driver killed it. She rounded the rear side of their SUV but stopped at the sight of the fawn behind their car.

Blood pooled underneath the fawn's carcass. Its head twisted to the side, its neck stretching like warped putty. Chloe winced as her stomach churned. Its lifeless eyes remained open, searching for the afterlife.

"Oh god." Chloe choked back a sob.

Philip rounded the SUV, approaching her with open arms. "It's okay. Shh, it's okay."

Chloe rested her head against his chest. The oak scent of Philip's cologne grounded her. Things could've been worse.

"Just an accident," he whispered into her hair.

She wiped her tears against his shirt. "It was so young."

He rubbed her back and tried to quiet her worries. "I didn't mean to hit it." Philip's chest rose and fell as he let out a heavy breath. "And death isn't ageist."

Chloe pressed her hand against his chest, breaking their embrace. She searched his eyes, taken aback by his matter-of-fact attitude. But of course he would need to compartmentalize death; he was a doctor.

"Holy spit!" A man climbed out of the cab of his red truck. "That som'a bitch jumped out right in front of ya." He had a beard as thick as the forest and he shuffled toward them.

Philip walked away from Chloe and met the man between the cars. Their hands collided, clasping together in a firm shake.

"I tried to dodge it," Philip explained. "You'd think I wasn't raised up here with those things crossing the road all the time."

"Livin' down in those cities will do that to ya, Philly," the man said. In a town of only a few hundred people, of course Philip knew the man. He nodded his chin toward Chloe. "Miss, are ya okay?"

"I'm fine," she replied. "Just a little on edge."

"Rusty, this is my fiancée, Chloe," Philip explained.

The old man smoothed his beard. "Welcome to Hallowed Pines. Nice to meet ya."

Chloe forced a smile, still tense from the accident. She rested her hip on the side of their car. "What should we do? Call the police?"

The older man barked out a laugh. "Oh, I'm afraid that's not going to be helpful, seeing as the closest law enforcement office is more than thirty minutes away."

Chloe cocked her head and flashed a concerned look at Philip.

He acknowledged her with a nod. "Rusty, what about the fire department?"

The old man adjusted his belt. "You mean the one that got shut down two years ago? We've only got a few of us who volunteer up here and you're lookin' at one of 'em right now."

A chill snaked down Chloe's spine. The lack of resources in a town nestled in the forest forced her to consider the overall remoteness of the area. There was no way in hell she could ever live like this.

Rusty waved at an incoming car as he and Philip discussed their car's damage. She drowned out most of their conversation, catching only pieces: something about their alignment being off; the bumper needing some-such repair; a cracked headlight lens. She glanced at the young deer. This poor animal died, never to roam the forest again. Guilt pooled in her center. *All because I distracted Philip's driving.* Bile climbed up her throat as her stomach knotted. "I think I'm just going to walk the rest of the way."

Philip broke away from his conversation with Rusty. "Sweetie, are you sure? I don't know if it's a good idea for you to be al—"

"I told you that I'm fine," Chloe assured him. She pointed toward the road. "It's not that far. Just a five-minute walk or so. The fresh air would be good."

Philip pressed his forehead against hers as he embraced her. "Okay. Just be careful. I can't let anything happen to you," he whispered.

She eased into his arms, not caring if the other man was watching. Philip loved her deeply and wanted her to be safe, no matter where she went. His desire to protect her at all times added another layer to their love. Another month and he would be vowing his life to her and she to him.

"I'll text you when I'm there," she said, pulling away from him.

She returned to the car and collected her cell phone and

purse. She glanced at the mess of her binder. She could fix that later. Right now, she wanted to get far away from the scene of the accident and shed the guilt that gnawed at her. Her new wallpaper was waiting.

She waved to the two men and set off. Their voices grew distant as Chloe walked along the side of the road. The sound of crunching pine needles underneath her sneakers became the rustic soundtrack to her journey. She breathed in the mountain air and smiled. At least she was getting her steps in.

As the road stretched and veered to the right, Chloe ventured down a beaten path. Gravel crunched under her shoes as she picked up her pace. As she walked down the private driveway, the silhouette of the steeple poked through the pine tree canopy. She passed a sun-bleached wooden sign that read "Hallowed Pines Gathering," the name of the former church Philip's family founded. The first time Philip brought her to Hallowed Pines, Chloe had joked that the name sounded more like a cult, than an evangelical church. The fact that the prior congregation only had thirty members provided further suspicions of what exactly went on in the building. Philip explained that their church had been different. That his grandfather's mission had been to create a *movement*.

"Like a former secret society," Chloe had laughed at the explanation, but Philip's stern look drained any suggestion that he was joking. And she'd been too nervous, and a little creeped out, to ask any more questions.

As the building came into full view, Chloe's heart brightened. She couldn't tell why, but when Philip first showed her the property, Chloe felt an immense fascination. Built in the 1930s, the roughly 1200-square foot building sat centered on the 20-acre plot of dense forestry. *A hidden gem,* she'd told Philip on her first visit. She valued the vacant space for its potential. An opportunity to showcase her craft of revitalizing the forgotten into something memorable. Determined, Chloe was set to transform this former church into a wonderful ranch-style home.

As Chloe stepped onto the porch, the scent of fresh paint greeted her. She cocked her head, examining how the sunlight illuminated the new shiplap walls. The color turned out to be more yellow than she had intended. Her chest pinched, wishing she could have confirmed the painters had used the right hue.

Fuck it, Chloe thought. *It's close enough.*

She fumbled through her purse and pulled out a set of keys. Reaching for the doorknob, she froze. Fear pricked the back of her neck, tugging her back a step.

The front door swung open on its own.

Two

The floorboards creaked underneath her. She forced down a gulp, scanning the interior, discerning if someone else was inside the house. *Their* house.

"Hello?" Chloe's voice reverberated against the unfinished walls of the old vestibule.

She gently set her belongings on the kitchen counter to her immediate right. Walking down the length of the galley kitchen, Chloe didn't notice anything out of place since their last visit two weeks ago. The same half-used roll of paper towels sat to the left of the metal sink. Two camp-style chairs remained folded, stacked against the laundry room door at the other end of the kitchen. She folded her arms across her chest as she entered the hallway.

"Hello?" she called out once more.

She waited for any sounds of movement, any clue that she was not alone in the house.

But none came.

She huffed as she walked back toward the front door. Closing it, she reengaged the two deadbolt locks. Pressing a hand against the wooden door, her mind rattled against her skull. How in the world did the door get left open? She and Philip always locked the door whenever they left. Living in the city had embedded the habit into their muscle memory. She looked out the small window on the right side of the door. Branches of pine needles swayed in the breeze. Could the wind have been responsible?

The scent of fresh paint, sawdust, and solvents eased her concern. Of course no one was here. The house was tucked away from the main highway, out of sight and out of mind. Instead, it could have easily been someone Philp hired who forgot to latch the locks. She turned back to face the open foyer, raking her teeth across her bottom lip. There was so much that still needed to be done. Worry pricked at her temples. The wedding was a month away, 28 days to be exact. The stress of renovations on top of wedding plans was making her paranoid. And if they didn't move faster, she'd have to face the fact that her ideal rustic wedding venue was going to resemble a construction site. The thought sent a tinge of unease down her spine.

She wasn't going to let that happen.

Her phone dinged. She pulled it out of her pocket and glanced at the text from Philip.

Rusty is going to tow us. Headed to the house.

She blew out a sigh of relief. At least they didn't have to wait for hours to try to find a tow truck to come up the mountain. She swiped away the message when another notification flashed across her screen: Two years ago today...Her eyebrows furrowed. An old photo filled the screen. The blurry, low-lit picture stole her next breath. Chloe recognized the man immediately.

Allen.

A man who wasn't just her lover—but also her former Human Center Design Principles professor. The phone shook in her unsteady hand. She was convinced she had deleted all photos from her phone, wiping away any trace of their relationship. Yet, this remained, displaying her wide smile and closed eyes, capturing a moment of pure bliss while the man with salt-and-peppered hair nuzzled her neck. If only his class and internship hadn't been required for her bachelor's in interior design degree. She would've never had been entangled in a forbidden affair.

"Allen," she whispered to herself.

Her fingers frantically clicked on the trash icon. She double-checked her phone's gallery to ensure the image had been deleted. But she couldn't deny the piercing agony in her heart. Allen had been erased from her life. Guilt flooded her body, pooling like thick tar between each of her bones. *He's dead because of me*, she reminded herself.

Shoving her phone into her back pocket, she bit the side of her tongue, refocusing on the present moment. Allen had passed away more than a year ago, and she was engaged to Philip now. Dwelling on the past wasn't going to change it. She needed to move forward with her life.

Walking through the foyer, she followed the freshly polished floorboards to the new living room. Two sheets of plastic draped across the hallway frame like theater curtains. Peeling back the plastic, Chloe took in the view of the large space that used to be the sanctuary.

Gone were the pews that had lined the center of the room. The steps to the altar led to a raised dining area, erasing any memory of this being a house of worship. Through their renovations, Philip and Chloe had transformed the Sunday school room and pastor's office into two bedrooms, complete with a galley-style kitchen, a master bathroom, and a laundry room. Now, the expansive space where the congregation used to meet resembled more of a slender, long ballroom. She chuckled to herself as she tried to imagine Philip waltzing her around the room for their first dance as husband and wife. He readily admitted he was born with two left feet. Still, she couldn't help but hear the notes of a piano playing in her mind as she imagined what their first dance would look like.

Closing her eyes, she could hear the musical notes of a soft melody. But an unfamiliar tune interrupted her reverie. Her eyes popped open as somber tones, all the minor keys in *C, D,* and *E,* filled the entire house.

Someone was playing a piano inside the house.

Chloe tiptoed toward the bedroom on her left. The melody grew louder. The bedroom door, formerly the pastoral office, was cracked open only an inch or two. But Chloe could see the protective cloth peeled back, revealing the shiny lacquered wood of the piano wedged into the corner of the room.

An elderly woman with frizzy gray hair pulled back into a low bun sat on the bench, her fingers flying over the piano keys. Her head bobbed with the song. She closed her eyes and parted her lips. "He knows, he knows, he knooooowwwsss," she sang.

Fear clutched Chloe's heart. Even though the lady's small frame and frail skin dismissed the possibility of a life-threatening attacker, she didn't recognize the woman. Chloe pushed the door open farther as she stood in the doorframe, hoping the whining hinges would be enough for the elderly woman to notice she had been caught in a house that was not hers.

The woman's fingers stiffened as she lifted her hands from the piano. She raised her arms to the ceiling, dipping her head back. "He knows what you are and what you've done," she sang to the rafters.

"Hey," Chloe said.

The woman recoiled her arms as she turned in her seat. Her icy eyes fell onto Chloe. Her ruby-colored chapped lips, cracked into a smile, exposing her crowded, stained teeth.

The woman's cheery smile and blank stare rattled Chloe to the core. "I-I don't think you're supposed to be here."

The woman blinked. Her arms fell to her sides as her shoulders slumped. The wooden piano bench creaked underneath her shifting weight. "Oh my dear," the woman said. "We are *all* welcome in the house of the Lord."

Chloe shook her head. "No, this isn't a church. Not anymore. And you're trespassing. I'm going to have to ask you to leave. Is there someone I can call to come take you home?"

The elderly woman rose from the bench, her intense gaze fixed on Chloe. "You need to start repenting for all you've done, defiling this place of worship."

Anger heated Chloe's skin. Her politeness dissolved. "Get out now or I'm going to have to call the..." Her voice trailed as she recalled Rusty informing her the police were more than half an hour away. *God, where was Philip?*

The elderly woman chuckled as she walked toward Chloe. Smoothing her wool skirt, the woman stepped closer. The scent of musk and vanilla failed to mask the ammonia stench flooding Chloe's nostrils. The woman raised a slender finger, pointing at the wall.

"These souls will not be able to rest if you don't stop what you're doing," she warned.

Chloe took another step back, welcoming the expansive space the living room brought. She kept her focus on the elderly woman who began humming. Chloe pointed toward the door as fear stripped her of any words. The woman nodded, then rushed toward the front door.

Metal scraped as the woman undid the locks. Fresh air flooded the house, carrying the scent of the woman's perfume. The elderly woman raised a finger toward the sky and opened her mouth.

"He knooooowwwsss," she sang.

Three

G ravel crunched under tires. A diesel engine rattled through the air. Chloe stopped pacing the porch and breathed a sigh of relief.

Philip.

Her fiancé hopped out of the cab of Rusty's red truck towing their SUV. Chloe bounded off the porch steps and rushed to Philip. She wrapped her arms around his torso, burying her face in his chest.

"There was someone here. There was someone in our house," she said through shaky breaths.

He clasped her shoulders and gently pulled her away from his chest. "Wait, someone was here? Inside the house?"

Chloe bit her lip as she recalled the strange woman. Her haunting song rang through Chloe's mind. She didn't know who the woman had been referring to, but something about how the woman had warned her, shook Chloe.

"There was this elderly lady," she said. "She was in our house, playing the piano and singing."

Philip squeezed her shoulders, dipping his head lower to meet her gaze. "Is she still inside?"

"No." Chloe locked her eyes with his. "Philip, she said some really creepy shit. Something about us disturbing souls. You locked the doors last weekend, right? Before we left?"

"Of course."

Chloe turned to face the house. "Then how did she get in?"

The truck door opened, pulling their attention to Rusty. "We better get going to my shop, Philly. The faster we get there, the sooner I'll be able to order parts and get ya fixed up."

Philip laced his fingers through Chloe's. "Come on. Let's go to town so Rusty can look at our car. We need to get some groceries anyway."

Chloe nodded. Making a trip into town was better than being stuck at the house alone, especially if the old woman returned. "Okay."

The ten-minute drive to the center of Hallowed Pines seemed to take about an hour. Most of that was due to the elaborate stories Rusty told Philip, updating him on the town's gossip. Chloe tried to fold herself up. Being stuck in the middle of the bench seat of the truck cab didn't help.

"Oh, and the Bensons decided to sell their house too," Rusty said.

"The Bensons?" Philip leaned forward. "To go where?"

"Oregon." Rusty huffed. "Crazy, right? Seems like no one wants to stay here anymore."

Chloe picked at the fabric of her pants. "But not you, huh?"

Rusty sucked his teeth. "Miss, I was born here, lived here my whole life, and will die here. Nothin's changing that."

Chloe was relieved their conversation was cut short as the truck turned onto Main Street. They drove under a large timber archway with a carved sawblade depicting the town name, HALLOWED PINES, in the center. Tiny shops had been wedged together on a single road, though most of the buildings seemed vacant. Small groups of people gathered outside of the post office, fixated on conversation. The truck pulled into the Hallowed Pines Market parking lot.

"You two stay safe and clear from those pesky deer," Rusty said with a nod.

"Thank you, Rusty. For everything," Philip said as he helped Chloe out of the truck cab.

"Anything for the Blackwells," Rusty replied with a wink. "Anything."

Once out of the truck, Philip slapped the truck door twice, relieving Rusty from his chauffeur duties. Chloe crossed her arms. "Interesting guy," she confessed.

Philip grinned. "Rusty may seem like a rough guy, but he's always been very helpful to my family."

"So, you've known him a while," she asked.

Philip plucked his glasses from his nose and wiped the lenses with the hem of his shirt. "His family has been in Hallowed Pines longer than mine. He used to be part of our congregation, our own handyman, if you will. So yeah, I've known him quite a while."

Chloe gripped her purse strap. "How come I didn't meet him the past couple of trips we've been here?"

Philip raked his teeth across his lower lip. Exhaling, he slid his glasses back into place. "He's the kind of guy who doesn't like to socialize much. However, he's always been there when my family needed him, almost like he has a sixth sense. Honestly, he's the nicest guy. He'd give the shirt off his back to anyone in need."

Chloe scrunched her face. "I'm not so sure I'd want it."

Philip chuckled as he wrapped an arm around her shoulders. "Let's go see if they finally have your favorite chips."

The market's doorknob bell chimed as they entered. They were greeted by a young woman who stood next to the single register. With her long straight hair pinned back by glittery pins and her face devoid of makeup except lip gloss and mascara, Chloe believed the girl must be barely of legal driving age. A few people flocked to the deli in the back of the store, caught up in conversations about getting ready for fire season and green waste burn days. Chloe picked up a wire-framed basket and plucked items from the shelves.

During renovations, Chloe decided it was best for the two of them not to rely on a full kitchen for their meals. Instead, she opted for items that didn't need cooking. Philip initially resisted the idea, getting sick of salads and peanut butter sandwiches, but relented because he knew Chloe was right. There was no need to bring pots and pans, dishes, and glassware. Their only reason for visiting was to get the house ready for the wedding and then put it on the market so they could finally focus on their future in the Bay Area. Chloe joked that it was their unique way of camping.

"Aha!" Philip exclaimed, rounding the corner of the bread aisle.

Chloe chuckled and followed him to the next aisle. "What'd you find?"

Philip snatched up the bag of pork rinds. "See, I knew they would order some after I said something last time."

Chloe folded her arms. The shopping basket rested on her hip. "Aww, that's so sweet." She took the bag from Philip and glanced over the packaging. "It's just not the same as back home. The one with the extra spicy flavoring."

Philip huffed. "Aren't they all the same? I mean, they're basically sodium bombs that no one should be eating."

Chloe placed the bag of pork rinds back onto the shelf. "It was a good try." She gave his arm a squeeze. "Don't worry, I'll pick up my own sodium bombs on our way back to the city."

"Deal," he said with a nod.

Her phone buzzed in her pocket. She pulled it out of her jeans and grinned at the text message from her best friend and wedding planner. "Oh, Harper is going to make it up here tomorrow with my dress. I can't wait."

Philip smiled at her. He turned his attention past Chloe and his eyes went wide. "Oh my gosh, Lorraine?"

"I thought that was you!"

Chloe turned around to see a middle-aged woman wrap her arms around Philip's torso. Every time they visited the mountain town, Chloe was reminded that she was about to marry a local celebrity. The small-town boy who moved to the city and became a praised pediatrician. Not Oscar-worthy, but Chloe couldn't help the pride she felt slipping her arm between his in this town.

"How's Mitch and the tree trimming business going?" Philip asked, lacing his arms across his chest. "Oh and the boys? I bet they're so big by now."

Lorraine beamed. "Oh, they're just as good as I hope heaven to be. There are still plenty of trees to cut down, what with the power company demanding more and more timber to fall. And the boys are both in middle school now."

Philip grinned. "My gosh, already? I remember when they used to come to Sunday school."

Chloe noticed other customers peeking down the aisle. The sudden weight of stares pressed against her back. Looking down, she glanced at Lorraine's cowboy boots, then stared at her own satin ballet flats. Hushed murmurs reminded her that she was a stranger to this small town. She took hold of Philip's wrist and passed the grocery basket to him.

"I'm going to run to the bathroom," she announced. "They do have one, right?"

Lorraine nodded to the left. "Straight back there past the deli counter."

"Thanks. I'll be right back," Chloe said and left the two of them in the middle of the snack aisle.

The scent of vinegar and salted meat lured her toward the deli counter. Following the hallway, Chloe found the single-stall bathroom. She flicked the light switch on, sending a buzz through the air as fluorescent light spilled into the bathroom. After closing the door behind her, she rested her hands against the edge of the sink. Looking at her reflection, she pursed her lips, dissatisfied with how frizzy her hair was at the middle part.

"Just a few days here," she told herself as she turned on the faucet. Traveling up and down the mountain had become a chore. But a necessary one if she was going to showcase her design skills, a perfect opportunity to utilize the experience to attract design clients.

Patting her dark brown hair, she hooked loose strands behind her ears. Once satisfied, she shut off the water and smiled in the mirror. Blowing out a breath, she pulled a paper towel from the dispenser to dry her hands, then tossed it into the trash. She didn't need to fit in here, not when her time in this small town was so temporary.

Chloe opened the door and turned the light switch off. She walked down the hallway but was stopped by the stares of three children.

Bold lettering in the header depicted MISSING CHILDREN, with a description of each child:

TRISTIAN ANDERSON: Age: 6, Brown hair, blue eyes. Missing Since 04/22/2010, Last Seen in Hallowed Pines
AMELIA LARSEN: Age: 7, Blonde hair, green eyes. Missing Since 04/23/2010, Last Seen in Hallowed Pines
BRITTANY BISHOP: Age: 11, Brown hair, blue eyes. Missing Since 04/24/2010, Last Seen in Hallowed Pines

Chloe studied their faces, her heart breaking. All of them had gone missing a few days from each other. She traced her fingertip along the bottom of the flyer and pondered what could have happened. So much time had passed.

She decided not to let her imagination conjure gruesome scenes. Maybe one day they would be found, grown up now, and living a better life with greater opportunities away from this mountain. Still, her heart sank as she realized that even in such a small town horrific crimes such as missing children were inevitable.

Chloe returned to find Philip still chatting with Lorraine. She wedged herself next to Philip and offered her hand. "I'm Chloe, by the way."

"Nice to meet you," Lorraine said with a wink. "Say, aren't you two getting married real soon?"

"Twenty-eight days, to be exact," Chloe chimed in.

Lorraine placed a hand over her heart. "Oh, isn't that wonderful? I can't believe Philip has grown into such a handsome young man." She twisted the locket on her necklace. "You know, I think maybe my invitation got lost in the mail."

Philip forced a smile as he glanced at Chloe. "Oh, I'm sorry to hear that. I'll make sure my mother sends one as soon as they get back home from their trip."

"That'd be delightful. It was good to see you." Lorraine patted Philip's shoulder as they shuffled out of the aisle.

Chloe scooted next to him. "You're inviting another person to the wedding now? Babe, Harper is almost done with all of the wedding plans, and I told her we weren't having more than twenty-five guests."

"No, I'm not going to really invite her," he whispered. "I'll make sure her other invitation just so happens to get 'lost in the mail' as well." He emphasized with air quotes.

Chloe gasped, surprised that he would lie. "You, sir, are quite deviant."

"I'll repent later," Philip replied.

Repent.

Chloe shivered, the word hitting her like a blast of icy air. She thought back to earlier with the strange woman in their house and her warning to repent for the renovations. *Repent.* But could she have meant more? Did the old woman somehow know Chloe was hiding dark secrets from her past? The image of Allen's picture surfaced. *He knows,* the woman had sung. Another chill raced down her spine.

"You know what," Chloe said, picking up the bag of off-brand pork rinds. "I think these are exactly what I need right now."

As she set them inside the basket, Chloe paused for a moment as a familiar scent wafted down the aisle. She pinched her nostrils shut as the pungent aroma of ammonia sailed through the air.

"Oh, Callie!"

She turned at the sound of the woman's raspy voice. The elderly woman who had been in their house rushed down the aisle, abandoning her shopping cart.

"Thank the heavens you're all right," she barked. The woman reached for Chloe, tugging at her sweater. "I haven't seen you in so long. Are you hurt? You haven't been to church, and I was starting to get worried!"

"I'm not—" The woman's icy hand clasped over Chloe's lips.

"You don't know how worried I've been," she whined. Her frail arm shook as Chloe tried to pry herself free. The woman's grip tightened, forcing her fingernails into Chloe's skin.

"Miss Bonnie," Philip said, taking hold of the woman's forearm.

Chloe sucked in a fresh breath of air as the woman let go of her face. She noticed people staring. "I'm not Callie."

Philip took hold of Miss Bonnie's wrists. "Your cats—Miss Bonnie, you need to get home to your cats. They're probably so hungry."

The elderly woman blinked rapidly. She covered her mouth as she choked back a sob. "Oh my goodness, you're right! My poor babies are probably starving."

Chloe watched as the woman turned and shuffled back to her cart. Conversations resumed around them as if the whole incident had never happened.

"What the hell was that all about?" Chloe whispered.

Philip took the basket from her. "Miss Bonnie...she's had a hard time ever since her husband passed away several years ago. She started showing signs of dementia. When our church closed doors due to declining numbers five years ago, she had an even harder time. That was her excuse to be social, you know? Now she's got a whole feral cat population keeping her busy."

Chloe nodded, understanding the ammonia stench now. She rested her hand on Philip's shoulder. "But she thought I was someone named Callie?"

He huffed out a breath and cleared his throat. Adjusting his glasses on his nose, he flashed an awkward smile. "Callie was an old girlfriend of mine. You two look similar, so she just got confused."

A million questions flooded Chloe's brain. In all the times that they had visited Hallowed Pines, not once had the name Callie come up in conversation. Before she said a word, Allen's face flashed in her mind. So they both had secrets.

There was no use digging up the past now.

Four

Soft light bloomed from the vaulted ceiling. Philip's chewing echoed against the walls of the barren room. The metal legs of the camping chair creaked as Chloe adjusted her weight. The peanut butter soured in her mouth. As expected, the off-brand pork rinds made matters worse. She plucked clumps of bread from her sandwich, rolling the pieces into tiny balls next to the subpar pork rinds on her paper plate. The old woman's words still stung, infecting her with venom like a snake, wiping away any appetite.

"Hey," Philip said, resting his hand on top of hers. "Are you okay?"

Chloe licked her lips. "I'll be fine. There's just a lot going on. We're going to finish this all on time, right?"

He squeezed her hand. "Of course, or we'll die trying."

She couldn't hold back a smile. Philip was always good about cheering her up, even when a creepy lady seemed to be stalking her in a small town where she didn't belong. She lifted his hand and placed his fingertips across her bare shoulder. "You know, I am a little tight here. It's probably from being wedged in the middle on the way back in Rusty's truck."

Philip wiped his hands with a napkin and motioned for her to scoot closer. "Come here, doctor's orders."

She shifted her weight, turning her back to him. She pulled her hair aside and sucked in a breath as the cool night air spread across her exposed skin. Philip's hands went to work, tenderly massaging her flesh. She eased into his motion, feeling her muscles relax until she was soft as putty. She closed her eyes. "*Mmm*, that spot right there."

Philip's breath tickled. "Right here?"

She felt his hand slide down her back, underneath her shirt. His warm touch melted away the worries of the day. They could get through anything. They *would* get through anything—together.

Crack! Chloe straightened, dropping her hair back over her shoulders. "What was that?"

Philip shot to his feet. He glanced at the ceiling and scanned the rafters. "Probably just a temperature change," he offered with the slightest crack in his voice. He turned back toward Chloe, lending an outstretched hand.

She clasped his hand and stood. "Guess I'm jumpy from everything today. Maybe we should go to bed and rest. We can start on things early in the morning."

Philip planted a kiss on her forehead. "That sounds perfect."

Chloe turned and scooped up their paper plates, the weight of the day urging her to get rest. After throwing away the trash, she walked to the primary bedroom and stopped in the doorway. Not hearing Philip's footsteps behind her, she turned around.

"What are you doing?" she asked.

"We're not married yet," Philip said as he rose from his seat. He wedged himself past Chloe and tapped the door-frame. "My parents wouldn't approve of us sharing a bed."

Chloe forced a smile. "Your parents are on the other side of the country. There's a zero-percent chance they'll show up and catch us sleeping in the same bed."

"Chloe," Philip grumbled. "I know it seems stupid, but I'd like to honor my parents' wishes."

She rolled her eyes as a scoff spilled past her lips. "And back home when I stay the night at your apartment? We're going to act like that doesn't happen every other night?"

"Please," Philip whined. "It feels weird. I used to say my prayers crouched on this same floor."

"And when was the last time you prayed?" Chloe asked, crossing her arms.

"Okay, we're not going to do this again," Philip said, shaking his head.

"What?" Chloe took a step toward him. "I'm just trying to get a better understanding of what the rules are here. You know, a sinner like me who doesn't believe in organized religion doesn't understand all these boundaries."

"I don't either," he admitted. "But it's about respect—respect for my *family*. We don't need my grandparents rolling over in their graves."

"Fine," Chloe said, throwing up her hands. She marched toward the other bedroom across the living room. Her jaw clenched. If he wanted space, she was more than willing to give him some.

"I love you," he said.

"I love you too," she said over her shoulder. "Good night."

After brushing her teeth in the kitchen sink, Chloe

closed the door to the small bedroom. The narrow room only left room for a queen-sized bed and a small bedside table. She rounded the bed and plugged her phone into the charger, then set it on the bedside table. Climbing underneath the bedspread, Chloe didn't even bother to worry about changing her clothes. The drive had worn on her, the old woman's song still chilled her bones, and worst of all, she couldn't even have the safety of her partner's embrace to ease her into sleep. She turned off the bedside lamp and forced her eyes shut.

Sleep eluded her and after tossing in bed for what felt like an hour, Chloe grabbed her cell phone to check the time. Bright light flooded the sheets as she narrowed her eyes against the harsh light.

12:34 p.m.

She sat up on her elbows and looked out the window. The soft glow of the porch light illuminated the early spring grass being smothered by a layer of pine needles.

She refocused on her purse sprawled across the floor. Maybe she could be quiet enough that Philip wouldn't hear her. Maybe a little frigid air would remind her that sleep was better than worrying about all the things that needed to be done. She lay back down. Her stomach twisted into another rope of knots.

"Fuck this," she whispered.

She rose from the bed, slipped on an old hoodie, and plucked a lighter and a single cigarette from her purse. The steady rhythm of Philip's snoring reverberated from underneath the primary bedroom door, bouncing off the living room walls. *Good,* she thought. *He's fast asleep.*

As she opened the front door, cold air spread across her cheeks. She quietly latched the door in place and stepped onto the porch. Gravel crunched underneath her shoes as she walked toward the clearing. She pulled the hood over her head, tucking in loose strands of hair. She scowled at the cigarette; she hadn't done this in years. The last time she filled her lungs with nicotine was to cope with the burn of Allen's untimely death.

A death she caused.

Lighting the end, Chloe inhaled a sharp breath. Smoke trailed up the sides of her face. The burn of the smoke settled into her chest, and she coughed like she was twelve years old, smoking for the first time again. After a minute, the soothing effect of nicotine coursed through her body like a warm hug. The jagged thoughts pricking her mind with worry smoothed into a reasonable checklist for the next day: clearing the living room, washing the walls, and laying out the wallpaper all before Harper's arrival.

Crickets chirped in the distance. A light wind blew through the trees. She looked up at the dark sky and grinned. The days here were beautiful, but the starry nights were breathtaking. Satisfied, she snuffed out the cigarette in the dirt.

Worn door hinges whined in the air. Chloe gripped the cigarette butt and whipped around. *Shit, Philip will kill me.*

Seeing the front door still closed, Chloe sighed a breath of relief and looked at the cigarette butt in her hand. She dug a small hole in the dirt to bury her little secret beneath the forest floor. As her fingers raked the wet soil, something cold grazed against her hand.

The air curdled in her nose, smelling of rotting fish and decaying grass. *Something died here.* Chloe stopped digging and sat back. She had horrible luck; it should have come as no surprise she would pick the exact spot of a dead animal to dig. She shifted her weight, bracing herself for the creature's remains to become visible.

Mud-crusted fingers rose from the soil. Chloe froze, unable to take her eyes off the hand emerging from the ground. Slender fingers snatched her right wrist, constricting around her skin like a ravenous snake.

"Ahh!" Chloe screamed.

Decaying knuckle bones split through rotting skin as the hand squeezed. Chloe thrashed, digging her heels against the moist soil as she attempted to pry herself free. The foul smell intensified as the hand overtook, pulling her closer and closer to the ground. Losing her balance, Chloe whimpered as she was pulled against her will. Her face inched closer to the soil.

"Help!" Her desperate cry tangled with a sudden violent wind bending the limbs of the pine trees.

The cigarette butt fell from her hand as she tried to pry the other person's fingers from her skin. Tears stung her eyes when her cheeks skimmed the wet ground.

A guttural cry scraped her lips as she swung her body back. Locking her left hand around her right forearm, Chloe used all of her might to thrust herself backward. Her shoulders slammed into the ground.

Finally free, Chloe shot up to her feet and ran back toward the house, not daring to look behind her.

Five

R ough lips grazed her lower jaw. His beard stubble tickled her skin. Chloe arched against his touch. "Allen," she moaned.

"Shh," he whispered into her ear.

She caught his hand, stopping him from further caressing her neck. She swallowed hard, pushing away the desire to be closer to him. "We can't do this anymore."

Allen's jaw stiffened as he took a step back. "And why not?"

Tears flooded Chloe's eyes. His sharp tone twisted her insides, scolding her once again like she was misbehaving. "Because you're married. And you're my professor."

"That hasn't stopped you in the past three months, now has it?" Allen took a step forward, driving Chloe's back to the wall of the dimly lit closet.

His hands roamed over her blouse while he nibbled her earlobe. Chloe shook her head, tearing her skin from his mouth. "She knows."

The room went quiet. Allen's hot breath fluttered against

her neck. He looked at their feet as his breathing picked up in rhythm. Chloe reached out, trying her best to calm him. "I'm sorry, but I had to tell her the truth. We're through."

Allen cocked his head. His eyelids popped open, filling with pools of black ink. His hand wrapped around her wrist, squeezing tighter and tighter. Chloe winced in pain, struggling against his strength. As she looked down, her chest tightened. The flesh of Allen's fingers began to decay. Bile and blood seeped from the cracks of his knuckles.

Chloe jolted awake. A band of sweat coated her hairline. She sat up on her elbows. Sunlight spilled into the bedroom from the arched window. She scanned the bedroom, comforted by the disarray: strips of wallpaper and color swatches poking out of her binder. Allen wasn't here. He was dead.

An aching pain emanated from her right arm. Chloe glanced down. Mud stained her skin. The smeared handprint pulled her back into reality.

Dead.

She shot out of bed.

Rushing to the other bedroom, barbed wire tightened around her core. *How did I fall asleep?* She recalled racing back to the house, but she couldn't remember even opening the front door.

Chloe swung the primary bedroom door open. Darkness met her. "Philip, honey," she said. "There's something I have to show you."

The bedsheets twisted around the silhouette of his body. Shifting his weight, Philip repositioned himself with a groan. Chloe bit her lip. Philip didn't like to be woken up abruptly, especially when a cup of coffee wasn't within arm's reach. But she needed to show him what had happened last night.

Flicking on the light switch, Chloe rushed to the side of the bed. Philip grunted as he pulled the quilt over his head. "Sweetie, please. Give me five more minutes."

"I know it's early," she replied and shook his shoulder. "But I need you to get up. There's something outside you need to see right now."

Philip lifted the blanket from his head. "Something outside? Is everything okay?"

"I—I don't know." She rubbed her wrist, still feeling the residual sting of pain from the hand gripping her.

Philip rose from the bed, the quilt unraveling from his body and falling to the floor. He plucked his glasses from the nightstand, settling them into place before raking his fingers through his messy brown hair. He pulled on his cardigan and sat on the edge of the bed to put his shoes on. "Stay here."

Chloe refused. Instead, she followed him to the front door. Bright sunlight spilled onto the porch where they stood. Chloe pointed to the spot where she had tried to bury her secret. "Over there."

Philip covered a yawn with his hand. Their SUV was parked several feet away from the house. "Looks like Rusty was able to fix it overnight."

Chloe blinked. "I didn't even hear his truck."

"Guess we both got some good sleep," Philip said with a smirk.

Chloe hugged her elbows and watched him charge down the porch steps. He stopped for a moment, scanning the expansive landscape. He held out an open hand toward her, urging her to stay put. Cautiously, he approached the mound of dirt.

Philip bent down. She no longer cared if he found the cigarette butt; she needed someone else to see that there was something very wrong here. She caressed her wrist, recalling the tight grip from last night.

Philip cried out and stumbled backward. He buried his face into his elbow. He coughed hard and cursed.

Chloe jumped down the porch steps. She raced toward Philip as fear laced up her legs and settled in her core. He saw it. He had to have seen the hand.

"F-fucking hell," Philip stammered as he stood.

Chloe embraced him, comforted by his warmth. "See, I told you something was wr—"

The syllable collapsed in her throat. A putrid stench shot up to her nose, reeking like rotting shellfish. The hole she dug was still visible, but in the center, there wasn't a hand. Instead, a cluster of red tendrils were situated in the dirt.

Philip ushered her back toward the porch. "Go sit down. I'll take care of this."

"There was a hand," Chloe admitted. She motioned to her arm. "It came out of the ground like a fucking zombie and grabbed my wrist last night."

Philip turned around. "Last night? What were you doing out here last night by yourself?"

Chloe crossed her arms. "I couldn't sleep."

Philip pursed his lips. He looked over at the cluster of pine trees to the right. Then he pulled Chloe close to his chest. She fell into his embrace, thankful that he was there to protect her. He would protect her from anything.

"You were smoking, weren't you?" Philip sneered.

Chloe looked up. "I—yes." The admission stung. She was better than that, having quit years ago and understanding that Philip didn't approve of such habits. "But I'm telling you, there was a hand that reached out and—"

"Devil's fingers," Philip said as he broke their embrace.

"It's a fungus, not a real hand or a zombie. This is what happens when you don't sleep, sweetie."

Chloe wedged her tongue against her gums. Was it possible that the hand reaching out for her had been another bad dream? Her fingertips rested against her wrist.

No. The pain had been real.

"I'm going to run to the market and get some weed killer to deal with it. Want to come? We can get breakfast on the way," Philip suggested, starting for the house.

Chloe took in the landscape, carefully eyeing the house. Something was off. Messing with her dreams. No matter how tempting it was to leave the property, Chloe shuddered at the thought of the old woman coming back unannounced.

"I'll stay here," Chloe said as she caught up to Philip. "Maybe I need a little bit more sleep."

Rushing back to the bedroom, she tried to calm herself. It was just some damned fungus, not a hand. She felt so stupid. She thought of the dream about Allen, so maybe the stress had jumbled it all in her mind. There was no hand. Nothing had tried to come after her.

Finally, alone in her room, she scooped up her cell phone from the bedside table. She pulled up her Notes app and punched in the phone number for Culver's Construction. There was too much that needed to be done, and if they could at least have a contractor pick up wherever they left off after this trip, she would have the relief that the property would be ready for their wedding.

"Hello?"

She pressed the phone closer to her face. "Hi, my name is Chloe. My fiancé and I recently bought a property in Hallowed Pines that we could use some help with."

"Oh yes, of course. I'd be happy to help you and your

fiancé," the man said. He cleared his throat as he tried to hush a barking dog. "Where exactly are you located in Hallowed Pines?"

"The old Blackwell property. You know what used to be the Hallowed Pines Gathering church?"

The call ended.

Chloe cursed under her breath as she walked out of the bedroom and toward the front door. Shitty phone service was all too real on this mountain. Once on the porch, she dialed the number again.

"Hello?"

"Hi, this is Chloe again," she said in a cheery voice. "I'm sorry. I think we got disconnected. Anyway, about the property—"

"Miss?"

She paused. "Yes?"

The man clicked his tongue. "No one is going to come out to the Blackwell property. No one from around these parts will touch that place."

She furrowed her eyebrows and shook her head. "Why not?"

He cleared his throat. "Miss, I don't know how to tell you this, but that property needs to be left alone. It's far too much work for you to handle. For anyone, really."

"So, you're not even willing to come out and give me a quote?"

There was a long pause at the other end. Chloe had to look at her screen to ensure their call hadn't been disconnected again.

"Miss," the man said, lowering his voice. "There are some things that are not worth fixing, you know what I mean? And the Blackwell property is just that."

The call ended again. Chloe scoffed and shoved her phone in her pocket. *Screw him,* she thought. *I'll do it myself. No one will touch that place.*

A chill raced down her spine. Why would no one touch this place?

Six

~~~

C hloe scoffed at the words of the contractor. Why were all these people trying to warn her about this place? Did they all believe they were upsetting souls by touching it, as if it were built on sacred ground? Given the history of the entire town, no doubt the construction company had worked on buildings with tragic backstories. *They* may be afraid of dismantling the old church to make way for a better future; Chloe was not. After all, even Philip's parents admitted that a building doesn't make a church, its people are the body or something to that effect.

Motivated by the man's doubts, Chloe got to work. She laid drop cloth over the wooden floorboards and rolled out sheets of wallpaper. She filled the room with her classical music playlist, then set her phone in a plastic cup. The melodies drowned the worry, alerting her to pack up and leave the house, that pricked at her conscience. Instead, she picked up her pace, making careful cuts and laying out the pattern on the living room floor.

Once the supplies were gathered, she poured the liquid

glue into a plastic container and readied the paint roller. As she doused the roller, Chloe accepted that Philip may be upset that she started without him. But she needed to do something, anything to speed up the decorating process and transform this house into a home.

She lathered the wall with the sticky paste, trying her best not to make a mess and add more work to her project list. A thin, shiny layer coated the wall. Chloe picked up the piece of wallpaper and carefully affixed it to the wall. Once satisfied with its placement, Chloe stood back and examined her work. She cocked her head to each side, placing her hand in the air for reference as she contemplated the positioning. With the ornate pattern, it was obvious the piece of wallpaper was placed too high on the right. She cursed as she rushed over to try and maneuver the paper into a better position. As she shifted her weight, the floor beneath her creaked.

Chloe felt a bump underneath her shoe, like she'd stepped on something. She shifted her weight. The floorboard groaned against her feet. She looked down and noticed a lip of wood protruding from the corner. She huffed, placing her hands on her hips. Of course, it was one thing right after another.

Chloe moved the supplies to the center of the living room. Peeling back the plastic cloth, Chloe examined the loose floorboard. She used the end of a flathead screwdriver to wedge the plank back into position. Instead of settling into place, the board popped completely free. As she picked it up, Chloe spotted a large piece of worn paper attached to the underside of the board.

She detached the paper and set the board aside. Chloe opened the letter. Elaborative cursive lettering spilled across the worn page.

Darling, I can't help but wonder if you are sick yourself. YOU MUST STOP. This is not the way you want to be remembered. You must think of the children and their future as well.

Her jaw tightened. The children? She turned the page over, hoping for more context. Not finding any, Chloe read the message again. "What happened?" she whispered.

The paper ignited, scorching the letters. Chloe gasped and dropped the note. The letter burned until there was nothing but bits of ash. She looked around the room as her breath became ragged. That's when she saw it.

Tendrils of black smoke poured into the room.

The stench of burning paper intensified as more smoke billowed into the living room. Thick clouds of smoke enveloped her, stinging her lungs.

Whispers and cries overlapped into muffled chaos, beating against her eardrums.

She covered her ears and made her way toward the front door, coughing up the billowing smoke along the way. But the air was too thick, stinging her eyes and robbing her of any chance of a fresh breath. The room swirled as blackness clouded her vision.

Indiscernible voices grew louder and louder, weaving together until they all began chanting as one.

"Who are you?" she asked through a shaky breath. She pressed her hands against her ears. "What do you want?"

WE FORGIVE SO THAT WE MAY ALSO BE FORGIVEN.

The chanting amplified, knocking into Chloe's skull like a sledgehammer. Smoke flooded her nostrils, catching in her throat as she had no choice but to suck in a harsh breath. She dropped her hands from her face and raced toward the front door. A white light burst through the doorframe. The black smoke stretched, spiraling like a tornado.

A dark figure appeared in the doorway.

Chloe screamed, then sank to the ground and allowed the darkness to take her.

Seven

"Chloe."

His voice sounded miles away. Yet her subconscious clung to its call, pulling her back to consciousness. "W-what?"

"Wake up. Please wake up."

Philip. She opened her eyes. He cradled her in his lap, smoothing her hair from her eyelashes. "Chloe?"

"I'm here. I'm okay," she assured him. Her focus pulled toward the ceiling. Not a single tendril of smoke could be seen. The air was full of dust and chemicals. But she knew down to her bones there had been smoke just a moment ago...right before she—

"What happened?" she asked, sitting up on her own. She glanced around, trying to find any remaining ash from the note that had burned. All of the flooring was intact, not a single piece out of position.

"I think you fainted." He smoothed her hair again, wiping his fingertips against her forehead. "I'm so glad you're awake."

"I remember putting that up," she said, pointing to the sheet of wallpaper. Its corner peeled over onto itself. She swallowed hard. "And then I—I don't remember anything."

"The fumes from the glue," Philip explained. He assisted Chloe to her feet and directed her to sit on top of their cooler in the middle of the living room. "Sweetie, I told you not to start without me."

Guilt swirled in her stomach. "I know, but I thought I could handle it. I've done wallpaper dozens of times without any problem."

"We'll get to it," he said, patting the tops of her hands. "But we need to make sure you're okay first."

Okay. Was she okay? Since coming back to the house, she had experienced one unexplainable thing after another. Philip had to be right: the mix of wedding plans, fumes, and erratic sleep were the culprit. "I'm fine," she said.

"Good, because she'll be here any minute," Philip said as he pulled a water bottle from the plastic grocery bag on the floor.

Chloe cocked her head. "Who?"

"Harper, remember?" Philip knelt and looked her right in the eyes. "Are you sure you're up for this? I can call her and ask—"

"No, it's fine," she said, waving his concern away. "I think the comfort of seeing my best friend is exactly what I need right now."

Philip nodded and twisted off the cap. "Agreed. Just make sure you stay hydrated. I don't need my bride-to-be passing out again."

Chloe snatched the drink from his hand and chugged. She licked her lips as she pulled the bottle away from her mouth. "Yes, doctor."

~

AFTER ANOTHER HALF HOUR, A CAR PULLED DOWN the driveway, tires ground against gravel. Two punctuated car horn honks made Chloe rush toward the front door. "Hey!" she called out.

The door to Harper's bright blue crossover SUV swung open. Harper jumped out of the driver's seat and rushed to the porch. "Finally made it."

Chloe hugged her friend, inhaling the rich lavender scent of Harper's jagged pixie cut. She pulled away and was relieved to see her best friend's smile. It was the slice of home she needed. "Where's Jazmyn?"

"Being a good girlfriend and staying home with my cats," Harper explained as she adjusted her knuckle rings. "Besides, I wanted some time alone with my favorite bride."

Chloe chuckled and nodded toward Harper's car with her chin. "I'll help you with your things."

The two unloaded Harper's bags, then made their way toward the house. Harper smiled at Philip waving from the field. "What's he up to?"

"Weed control," Chloe said. She looked over at Philip. A chill went down her spine as she recalled the hand wrapping around her. No, it wasn't a hand. Just disgusting fungus.

Chloe led the way to the bedroom, setting Harper's things on top of the queen mattress. Harper praised how far the house had come in the few short months since the renovations had begun. But Chloe kept her gaze on the windows, staring out at the expansive forest surrounding the property.

"Jesus, are you all right?"

Harper's words pulled her attention back inside the house. "What? Yeah, everything's fine. It's just..."

"Chloe, spit it out." Harper sat on the corner of the bed. "I've known you for too long to know to not notice when something's wrong. I will force it out of you," she said.

Chloe sniffed and hugged her elbows. She looked around the small room. Harper had a knack for getting her to talk. Might as well be upfront. "I think I'm being haunted," she admitted.

"Haunted?" Harper furrowed her brows. "Who could be haunting you right now? This is one of the best times of your life. I mean, you're about to marry the man of your dreams and—"

"Allen," Chloe stammered. She connected her cold stare with Harper's. "I think he's trying to torment me for the way things ended between us."

Harper looked around the room and leaned forward. "The professor is here?"

Guilt bubbled up Chloe's throat, souring her tongue. "Yes, him. Of course, him. I'm the reason he's dead."

"H-hey," Harper stammered. "We've gone over this. You're not the reason Allen is dead. Allen decided that for himself."

"But I'm the reason he decided to..." She couldn't finish the sentence and solidify the harsh truth.

Harper took Chloe's hand in hers. "Chloe, we all are responsible for our actions and our actions *only*. Yes, you had an affair with him, but after you called it off, it was *his* choice to take his own life. That is not your fault, you understand?"

Tears rolled down the sides of Chloe's face. She acknowledged her guilt for Allen's death, the way it clawed at her insides every time she regretted having an affair with a married man. But she had to accept what Harper was saying. Having a future with Philip meant leaving the past behind.

However, replacing the resounding guilt and shame with the truth felt like placing a band-aid over a gunshot wound, messy and impossible.

"Hey, I have something to show you to get your mind in the right place," Harper said, rising from the bed.

Chloe blinked away her tears, wiping her nose on her sleeve. "What's that?"

Harper grabbed one of her suitcases from the stack at the end of the bed. She hooked the hanger to the top of the door and undid the zipper. Ivory fabric spilled out of the garment bag. Chloe gasped as she ran her fingers over the sweetheart-cut neckline. She fanned out the A-line frame of lace and organza material. The wedding may be about a month away, but this...this solidified the fact that she was no longer going to be Chloe Atchinson.

Instead, she was going to be Chloe Blackwell.

The fabric felt light in her hands. She let the edges of her dress fall from her fingertips as she took a step backward. She wanted to see the gown in all its glory.

But her breath caught in her throat. Her wedding dress floated toward the ceiling.

Eight

C hloe couldn't believe what she was seeing. The dress was suspended in the air right before her. She kept her eyes on the fabric and reached for Harper.

"Look," she whispered.

Harper's breath cut short. She leaned into Chloe's side, her lavender scent pooling in the air between them. "What the hell?"

Chloe stepped forward. Her quivering hand reached for the dress. If she could grab the fabric, even graze it with her fingertip, she would know she wasn't dreaming.

"Chloe, stop," Harper hissed.

She ignored her friend's warning. Curiosity pricked her mind.

She had to know.

Her fingers glided over the lace. The fabric warmed under her touch, growing hotter and hotter until her skin scorched. Red flooded her vision, painting the entire bedroom a crimson hue.

Crack!

Blood splattered across the dress. The dress fell onto Chloe's shoes. She screamed as she stepped back from the bloody garment, bumping into Harper. The two women shrieked as they raced out of the bedroom and into the living room. Chloe led the way toward the front door. It swung open before she could grab the doorknob.

Philip stood in the doorway; his eyes wild with concern. "What? What is it?"

"There's something in the bedroom," Harper blurted.

"We need to go now," Chloe said as she pushed against Philip's arm.

Philip rounded Chloe, keeping his focus pinned on the bedroom. She grabbed Harper's hand and watched her fiancé enter the room. She closed her eyes and waited for Philip's shock when he found the bloody wedding dress.

Her bloody wedding dress.

"Oh my god," Philip called out.

Chloe and Harper charged forward, bounding over tools and the wadded-up drop cloth. Chloe gripped the door-frame. Philip turned around with the wedding dress in his hands.

Only there wasn't a single drop of blood on the fabric.

"How could you do that?" Philip scowled. "I wasn't supposed to see this until our wedding day, at the altar." His eyes fixed on Harper. "Was this your idea?"

Harper scoffed. "What? No. Philip, I'm telling you that thing was in the air and then it—"

Chloe examined her hand. Her fingertips remained unscathed, not a single cut visible. The blood on the dress was not her own. Looking up, she despised how upset Philip looked at he met her gaze. She couldn't let him know the truth. She couldn't spout off another claim about a supernatural occurrence. What would he think of her? "It was my idea."

The two of them faced Chloe. Philip cocked his head. "Why would you play a trick on me?"

Words overlapped in Chloe's mind. She needed to come up with something fast, so she wouldn't stumble and blurt out what she and Harper had really seen. "I wanted to get your opinion on the dress, now that it's finally done."

Philip narrowed his eyes. "But sweetie, I'm not supposed to see—"

"Me in the dress," Chloe corrected. "There's nothing against the tradition of seeing the dress until our wedding day. So, what do you think?"

Philip licked his lips as he considered her words. Chloe shot Harper a serious look, begging her with a stern stare to go along.

"I think seeing it now will make it more real," Harper added. "You know, for knowing how the zipper works in the back."

"Harper," Chloe whined. "Please."

"It's wonderful," Philip said, setting the dress down. "But I really need to finish up out there before it gets too dark."

"Of course," Chloe said. "Sorry we distracted you."

Philip headed back outside. With the door closed, Harper pulled Chloe away from the dress. "What the hell was all of that? Why didn't you tell him?"

"Please," Chloe said. "I can't tell him any more about what is happening, not until we know more." She closed her eyes for a moment, picturing the look on Philip's face if she were to tell him the truth. Would he think she was going mad and they should go back home? Part of her tugged at that suggestion. Maybe that would be best. For all of them to go back to the city and try to get someone else to finish the renovations before the wedding. But a chilling thought snaked its way into her mind. If Philip suspected she was unwell, would he call off the wedding? Or worse, would that be the end of them? She opened her eyes and shook her head. "We can't tell him anything."

"I saw what you saw," Harper admitted. "There *is* something or someone here trying to tell you something. Seriously, how many horror movies start with shit like this? If we don't get to the bottom of this, I'm not so sure these messages aren't going to become more physical."

Chloe's core twisted. "Physical?"

"Yes, I don't know exactly, but there seems to be something trying to prevent the wedding from happening. We saw *blood*. On *your* dress."

Chloe couldn't deny it. Her friend was right. "But how are we going to figure this out?"

Harper paced the room, sidestepping the bed and the wedding dress. "We do what we did as kids."

Chloe scoffed. "You can't be serious."

Harper placed her hands on her hips. "Dead serious.

Chloe shrugged. "What, like a séance?"

"Exactly."

She looked at Harper, waiting for the slightest crack of a smile. Instead, Harper's lips stayed in a straight line, unwavering. If holding a séance meant they could figure out if Allen was tormenting her, at least they would be one step closer to stopping the horror. "Okay, séance it is." She bit her lip and nodded toward the door. "But what about Philip?"

"We won't tell him," Harper suggested.

Chloe looked around the room and shrugged. "I guess that's one advantage of us sleeping in separate rooms."

Harper halted. "Shit, are you serious? He's still making you guys do that?"

Chloe folded her arms in front of her. "He doesn't want to disappoint his parents. Claims they would know just by walking in here."

"Okay, let's get the fuck away from that thing," Harper said, pointing to the wedding dress, "and head into town."

"Town?" Chloe rose from the bed. "Why?"

Harper grabbed her bag. "We're going to need supplies. And a whole lot of salt."

Nine

After another dinner of peanut butter sandwiches, Chloe collected the paper plates before tossing them into a garbage bag hanging from the laundry room door by the kitchen. She returned to the living room and sat back down next to Philip who was listening to Harper tell another story about traveling to Thailand.

"I kid you not," Harper said, waving her arms in the air, "that if you even *think* you can handle spicy food, you will literally have your ass handed to you in Thailand."

"Yikes," Chloe said. "That's one heck of a mental image, Harper."

Philip sighed as he finished his bottle of orange juice. "She might be on to something though. I remember a night shift in the emergency room where a teenage boy ate a pepper on a dare. Poor kid ended up with severe anal leakage."

"Jesus," Chloe said, covering her ears. "This is the last time I get the two of you together."

Harper laughed as she tossed a wadded-up paper towel

inside the garbage bag. "Okay, enough about anuses. I think I'm ready to go to bed."

Chloe picked at her cuticles. Her skin buzzed with adrenaline, ready to try this séance at Harper's insistence. Only this wasn't a childhood sleepover. Even though she didn't really believe in calling on spirits, good or bad, this trip started convincing her that she should think otherwise.

"Yeah, I think I'm ready to turn in for the night too." Chloe turned to Philip and embraced him. "Sleep well."

Philip hugged her back, pulling her in close. When he finally let her go, he grazed her chin with his thumb. "I am so lucky to have you."

Butterfly wings fluttered inside Chloe. It was in these moments time stood still, enveloping her like a fairytale dream come true. They belonged together. With renewed motivation, Chloe planted a kiss on his lips, then stood.

"You two enjoy your girl time," Philip said as he folded up the camping chairs.

She followed Harper to the bedroom as her heart thrashed in her chest. Could this work? Chloe shut the bedroom door, then paced around the room. If Philip walked in on them performing a séance, she wasn't sure how he would react. She could hear his mother's voice: *Provoking the dead calls upon Satan himself.* But Chloe was desperate.

"You need to relax." Harper arranged candles on top of aluminum foil on the floor. She poured a line of salt near the doorframe.

"It's not that easy." Chloe said as she sat on the corner of the mattress. "Ever since we've gotten here, I feel like no matter what I try to do, everything is going to absolute shit."

Harper sat on the floor and pulled a lighter from her pocket. She lit each wick until the room bloomed with candlelight. The room transformed with the soft glow. Chloe huffed as memories flooded with the late-night talks she and Harper had on her bedroom floor as young girls. But this wasn't a night to talk about first crushes and grown-up goals. The image of the bloodied dress surfaced in her mind.

"What now?" Chloe asked.

Harper tapped on the empty space in front of her, urging Chloe to sit. "Now we call upon whoever the fuck is trying to tell you something."

Chloe nodded, still unsure about how all of this worked, if at all. "Okay, do your thing."

Harper blew out a breath and closed her eyes. Chloe followed her friend's lead and shut her eyes. Harper called to the spirit realm, claiming they meant no harm.

This has to work.

Icy air pricked the back of her neck, making Chloe sit up straighter. *Scratch. Scratch.* The rough scraping grew louder and louder, overpowering Harper's words. Her teeth chattered as her body quaked.

Thud.

Chloe dared to open her eyes.

Standing behind Harper, a woman raised her arm in the air. Below the elbow, the flesh was gone, only exposed bone remained. Her other hand gripped a saw as its teeth ground against bone.

"Harper," Chloe whined.

Her best friend opened her eyes and turned around. The woman sawing her arm vanished in a blink. Chloe stifled a scream, the cold stealing her voice entirely. Her mind was playing tricks on her. There was no one in the room with them. Chloe's mind wracked thought after thought, trying her best to kill any possibility that a ghost had been visible.

"You are not welcome here," Harper said in a low, stern tone. "You. Are. Not. Welcome. Here."

Chloe dipped her head, her gaze falling to her lap. At least Harper was with her. She wasn't alone. What was it that Philip had said? *When two or more are gathered...*

"You are not welcome," Harper sneered.

Chloe lifted her head. Her best friend's eyes glazed, white pooling into her irises until her sockets were the color of porcelain. A candle fell to Chloe's right, startling her as the melted wax splashed onto her knee. The face of the woman flashed in front of Chloe. Her jaw went wide as she held up her severed arm. Jagged bone caught Chloe's attention as the woman let out a scream.

Then the room went dark.

Chloe jumped up and clicked the light switch on. Her heartbeat thrashed violently in her chest as she rushed to her best friend. Harper's eyes popped open. The room warmed as if sunlight poured through the window.

"I think she's gone," Harper said with a smile.

Chloe swallowed hard and looked around the room. Harper was right.

Ten

The next morning, Chloe helped load up Harper's car with her belongings. For the first time on this trip, Chloe got a full night's rest. No more hauntings. Her wedding dress hung unblemished in the closet. Even with her restored sleep, she couldn't help shake the feeling that something seemed off with her best friend.

Chloe leaned against the car door, resting her forearm on the open car window. "Are you sure you have to go home now? You just got here."

Harper sucked her teeth as she adjusted her weight in the driver's seat. "I know I was planning on staying for at least another day, but Jazmyn needs me. She's worried one of the cats might be sick."

Chloe bit her lip. "Oh no, is it Finn?"

"Yep, so I see another expensive vet bill in my future."

"You promise to call when you make it home and let me know how Finn is?"

"Of course." Harper looked off toward the house, her brown eyes fixed on the closed front door.

Chloe pinned her attention on her friend. "Are you sure you're up for the drive today? I know last night was—"

Harper blinked. "We took care of *it*. Now you and Philip can go back to your renovations. I'll only be in the way. Plus, you know how Jazmyn is. She's not the best with animals."

Chloe pursed her lips. Usually, Harper stuck to whatever decision she made; there was no changing it. She was about to walk away when Harper snatched her wrist.

"Promise you'll sell this place," Harper sneered.

Chloe retrieved her arm from Harper's grip. "Shit, Harper. We will. Are you sure you're okay?"

Harper huffed out a breath and closed the driver's door. "I'm fine. I just miss Jazmyn and want to get the fuck off this mountain," she said out the open car window.

The engine roared to life as Chloe took a step back, waving goodbye to her friend. Chloe turned back to face the house. As much as she wished she could follow Harper, there was work to be done. Besides, the rest of the night had remained uneventful, without another trace of a ghost sighting. Maybe Harper's séance had worked its magic.

Back inside, Chloe helped Philip with minor repairs. The day was spent installing finish carpentry in the bathroom, updating outlets in all the rooms, and adding a fresh coat of paint to the kitchen. They both worked endlessly until it was time to break for a late lunch.

"So, what do you think?" Philip asked in between a bite of his peanut butter sandwich.

Chloe shrugged. "We still have to tackle the living room walls, but I think it's coming together. And we can say that we finished it ourselves. Forget hired hands."

"Just *tired* hands," Philip said before popping his last bite into his mouth.

Chloe wiped the corner of her mouth with a paper towel. Just a few more weeks and all of this would be worth it. The house would be finished, their wedding would be an enchanted day, and then they could move on to a new chapter together as husband and wife. She relished the idea, the dream lifting her spirit to the clouds.

Until Philip's phone rang.

He snatched his cell phone from his shirt pocket and examined the screen. His eyes went wide as he swallowed hard. "Hey, Mom."

Chloe's chest tightened. Were his parents already back from their trip and in town? She bit her lip as she looked around the living room. There was so much still to be done, too much for them to come for a visit. Chloe shot up to her feet, intent on making sure that Philip wasn't going to extend an invitation.

"Yeah, it's coming together." Philip flashed a grin toward Chloe. "What? No, of course things have been handled. Yes, I made sure to be careful. Oh? Back tonight?"

Chloe started waving her arms. No, they couldn't come tonight.

Philip picked up on her motions and nodded. "Mom, call me when you two get home tonight and we'll see what we're up to. Oh? Potato soup?"

Chloe huffed out a frustrated breath. Of course his mother would want them to come over to their place this evening. As much as Chloe loved Mrs. Blackwell's potato soup, she knew a visit meant they would not make steady progress.

"Yeah, yeah. That sounds great," Philip said with a smile. "Okay, love you too."

Chloe crossed her arms. "So, I guess we're not going to get to the wallpaper tonight."

Philip tucked his phone back into his pocket. "It's just wallpaper, sweetie. We can get it done in the next day or so."

Chloe collected her hair and pulled it to one side. "Yeah, but with your parents back home, I know that means they're going to be here every day. You know your dad's not going to sit by without helping, and what of his back? Didn't you say that it wouldn't be good for him to be moving around?"

Philip placed a fist on his hip. "They'll probably stop by, but you know my mother, she'll always come with some food. Aren't you sick of peanut butter sandwiches?"

"If peanut butter sandwiches are the key to us finishing this place in time, I'll gladly eat them."

Philip stood straighter. "Why are you so against my parents coming over? They have ties to this building too when they were serving as pastoral staff. They have every right to come over whenever they'd like."

Anger flooded Chloe's cheeks. "Fine. Let them come over. We'll have dinner and that will be a great time to tell them about how we're putting this place on the market right after the wedding."

Philip clenched his jaw. "Don't do that."

"Do what?" Chloe paced; her skin grew hot. "It's not my fault that you haven't told them."

"Oh, and it's all my fault, hm? I'm not the one who wanted all this elaborate work done. When I suggested we sell this place as is, or at least restored it back to how it was when my great grandfather built it, you threw a fit." Philip waved his arms in the air. "Oh no. We can't have it be classic farmhouse style. No, Chloe Atchinson wants to put her perfect touch on it. So we need to make it have fancy wallpaper and buyer-friendly colors."

Chloe furrowed her eyebrows. "Forgive me for wanting to bring some life into this forsaken church. It may have a solid foundation and good bones but it's nothing without—"

"Just be quiet," Philip cursed. "Gosh, are you trying to ruin everything we've been working so hard for?"

She took a step back. His soured tone and clenched jaw were too familiar. Allen used to raise his voice, get upset when she went on with her thoughts. She hadn't thought Philip was like him. But now, with his anger unmasked, Chloe couldn't believe she hadn't seen the familiar shade of red all along.

Philip scooped up the car keys from the small table. Chloe whipped around, following him to the front door.

"Where are you going?"

Philip halted, his hand resting on the doorknob. "Out. I'll be back later."

She jumped as the front door slammed behind Philip. She let out a sob before hot tears streamed down her cheeks. She should've stayed quiet, should've buried her thoughts into the depths of her being.

But it remained all too clear.

Chloe was alone. And if she didn't do something to fix it, she'd be alone forever.

Eleven

She rushed to the bathroom and splashed cold water on her face. The sudden change of temperature jolted her. She stared at her reflection.

Dark circles ringed her lower lids. Puffy, bloodshot eyes stared back at her. A bright shade of red colored the tip of her nose, and her hair looked greasy and disheveled. Yet, she needed more than a shower to fix this.

"Fuck this." If Philip could go and do whatever he wanted, she could too.

Chloe's stomped through the house to the living room. She threw down the plastic drop cloth, not caring if Philip walked in on her setting up to finish the last piece section wallpaper in the main room. If he wasn't so damn fixated on having a tantrum, he could be helping her instead of sulking God knows where.

She smoothed the wallpaper cuttings out onto the floor, aligning edges the best she could. As she worked, she reminded herself that she was strong, that she could overcome anything. Allen had tried to convince her she was nothing, that even with her love of decorating and hard-working demeanor, she always needed guidance—especially *his* guidance. Toward the end, she'd almost believed she couldn't be anything without him.

Then she'd met Philip.

She paused before picking up another piece of wallpaper. What had happened to Philip? What had their argument really been about? The sudden shift in his attitude wasn't something she had encountered before. Her mother's voice came to mind. *You haven't even been together for all four seasons. How could you possibly know that you love him?* For fuck's sake, was her mother right? Did Chloe really love him? She hadn't known him for that long.

She twirled her engagement ring around her finger and considered her mother's advice. If time were a true measure of love, then people wouldn't get divorced after being wed for so long. And what of the people generations ago who buried their secrets, tucking away the dark parts of who they were all the way down to their bones until their death, only to be discovered through other people going through their belongings? She slipped the ring off her finger, tucking it away in her pants pocket.

"Shh! Don't tell!"

Chloe froze. She waited for another whispered warning. She scanned the perimeter of the living room, settling her gaze on the front door. It remained shut; Philip hadn't returned.

"Peel to reveal."

She stood, trying her best to follow the voice.

Three small figures raced across the room, their footsteps pounding against the floorboards. Chloe blinked and stifled a sob.

"Peel to reveal," a child whispered again.

The hairs on the back of her arms rose with the goosebumps pricking her skin. She moved closer to the wall.

"Peel to reveal, Chloe."

Two girls and a boy stood before her.

She jumped back. Her chest heaved tight, sharp breaths. The air cooled. Her stomach clenched. She recognized them. Their photos. These were the missing children from the corkboard at the market. Their faces and dark eyes were almost an exact copy of the images.

But now they were in her house.

The boy pointed to the baseboard. A small corner of the old wallpaper revealed the underside of the wall. She crouched and ran her finger over the bent paper.

"Peel to reveal," Chloe repeated.

Digging a fingernail under the paper, she got a better grip. The section tore off abruptly, but Chloe sucked in a breath as she noticed the dark mark of a letter.

Curiosity overtook her. She tore chunks off the wall, discarding each piece. She stepped back to read the text sprawled across the wall.

WE FORGIVE SO THAT WE MAY BE FORGIVEN.
WE FORGIVE SO THAT WE MAY BE FORGIVEN.
WE FORGIVE SO THAT WE MAY BE FORGIVEN.

The phrase was everywhere. She took a step forward, noticing smaller text written between the lines of large text.

As God forgives, so will I, my love.
Always & Forever
P+C

67

Chloe's hand covered her mouth as she let out a yelp. Sweat collected at her brow. She ran her trembling index finger over the handwritten initials *P* and *C*. Those were her and Philip's initials. But before them, it was Philip and...

"Callie," she whispered.

This seemed like more than church history here. How long ago had this been written? She tugged another jagged line of wallpaper from the wall.

I KNOW YOUR SECRETS.

Her blood ran cold. Unlike the beautiful cursive, these words were carved into the wall. *Secrets*. Philip had mentioned small town secrets were never meant to be shared.

A flutter of black in Chloe's peripheral vision caught her attention. She turned and noticed a faint billow of white. Dozens of whispers flooded her ears, the words mixing together. Chloe shut her eyes to focus as she tried to understand what the voices were saying.

Her heart broke, these voices sounded like small children. Their cries and sobs overtook her consciousness. Her throat ached as she swallowed another sob.

"What do you want from me?" she asked.

But she couldn't understand them. Their voices overlapped, mushing into indiscernible chatter. But she couldn't ignore their screams.

Chloe spun around, dropping her hands to her sides. The weight of being watched pressed against her back. The heavy burden of the handwriting on the walls pressed against her heart as well.

Someone was with her.

Summoning strength, Chloe turned around. She hoped

Philip had returned, back with an apology and the comfort of his arms. Or maybe Harper came back to collect something she'd forgotten. She would even settle for Miss Bonnie, horrified as Chloe "defiled the house of the Lord," as the old lady warned.

But she didn't expect the woman who stood in front of her.

Chloe took a step back. The woman raised her sawed-off limb.

Oh my god, no.

The séance hadn't worked.

Chloe screamed.

Twelve

C hloe lifted her arms protectively out in front of her, trying her best to shield herself from the ghost approaching her. "Callie, stop!"

The ghostly figure dipped her head, lowering her limbs to her sides. Hope fluttered in Chloe's chest. Maybe she could reason with this spirit, make it go away on its own. Harper had said that sometimes spirits get caught between worlds.

But the ghostly woman let out a scream and charged forward.

A chilly blast smacked into Chloe. Her feet lifted from the floor as she soared backward against her will. She slammed into the wall, nearly knocking the wind out of her. The drywall crumbled and then Chloe found herself falling fast. Her limbs outstretched as she plummeted down faster and faster, too far down like Alice and her rabbit hole.

She collided against something hard.

Her vision went black. She couldn't move. *Shit, I'm paralyzed.*

Chloe tried her best to summon the strength to move her thumb. Any sign of movement meant she might be okay. When none came, she screamed.

Dots of colors emerged. Her head pounded as she searched her surroundings. The room seemed familiar, too similar to the living room she was just in. She couldn't make out where she was. Blueprints flashed in her mind. She sucked in a breath. This wasn't the living room.

This was the *original* Blackwell floorplan.

Four people gathered at the front of the large room. Lines and lines of empty pews sat behind them. The orange embers of candlelight bloomed and quivered as the strangers walked in a circle. Their voices came together as one.

"We forgive so that we may be forgiven," they chanted.

The words chilled Chloe. She'd seen the same phrase printed all over the wall. She couldn't wake up, couldn't will herself to see anything other than the scene that played out before her. She must be dreaming. Instead of fighting it, she gave way to her dream, allowing it to speak to her.

As the group continued in a circle, their paths widened. Chloe shrieked before she covered her mouth with the back of her hand.

No!

Three children lay next to each other, their eyes shut, their limbs sprawled across the floor. Their chapped lips and taut skin made it clear the children were not asleep—they were dead.

Voices continued to chant their forgiveness as one of them picked up a jagged-toothed saw. Try as she might, Chloe couldn't make out their faces. Instead, it seemed their eyes, noses, and mouths were blurred watercolors.

Then the awful scraping sound rang through the room.

Chloe heard herself screaming, but she couldn't make sense of how she'd gone back in time. The awful nightmare continued as she was forced to watch the group of people hack away at the dead children. Nausea roiled in her stomach. She willed herself to look away, unwilling to witness the horror in front of her. She closed her eyes and sobbed.

Her head throbbed. The painful images scraped against her skull. Chloe willed herself to open her eyes. Darkness overtook her vision. Above her a stark white light stole her attention.

Forcing herself up, Chloe was relieved as she planted her elbows against the ground. She escaped the gruesome memory. A memory that didn't belong to her.

The air was thick with dust and debris, causing her to cough whenever she took a breath. The ground was cold, much cooler than she remembered the house being. Panic swept over her body as she looked down.

Dozens of broken and chipped bones engulfed her lap. She couldn't tell if they were human, but the horrific images leftover in her mind persuaded her to get up and run. Chloe stumbled as she tried to plant her feet on the ground. As she reached for the light, her whole world swirled in a kaleidoscope of color.

She blinked and the faintest outlines of the living room came into view. All of it appeared far away, blurred by the pain pulsing through her skull.

The living room.

She sat up and immediately covered her forehead. Wet, warm liquid coated her hand. She pulled it away and examined her fingertips. Splotches of blood coated her skin. A dizzying nausea took over. She swallowed acidic bile and grabbed the exposed wooden frames for support.

Once she was back on her feet, she stumbled through the broken wall. She was relieved to be in the living room once again, away from the horror she couldn't make sense of. But what she couldn't escape was the mound of bones still stacked in the wall cavity.

She screamed once again, covering her mouth with the back of her hand. *It was real.* Not a phantom in a dream, not because she'd inhaled wallpaper glue, and not because her ex had died by suicide. *No.* A concavity filled with literal bones had been obscured by the old sanctuary wall, and it had nothing to do with her. She needed to get out and call the police. Needed to confront Philip.

Some secrets were meant to be hidden.

But she couldn't let this past remain buried, especially when she knew what had happened to those missing children.

Chloe staggered out the back door.

The remaining sunlight stabbed her eye sockets. Chloe's head pounded, distorting her vision, and stealing her breath. Her sneakers crunched against the pine needles as she looked around. Tall trees enveloped her, making her feel as if she walked in circles.

She needed to find help, get away from this haunted property, but the pain in her head overtook her. Collapsing, her knees bearing the brunt of her fall, tears poured down her cheeks. The images of the children twisted her stomach, pricking her core with panic and rage. She couldn't explain it, but she had been shown those horrible visions for a reason. Pulling out her phone, she unlocked the screen and dialed 9-1-1.

Only no one answered.

Chloe checked her phone—no signal. Rising to her feet,

she rounded the side of the house. If she followed the driveway down, she knew it would meet the highway. Then she could get help.

Her bloody fingers tapped the screen. She cursed as the call wouldn't connect. Her ragged breathing caused the pain to pound against her skull with every single step.

An arm encircled her torso. She screamed as the stranger's forearm pressed into her core, restricting her from escaping.

Her feet dragged through the gravel as she was hauled back against her will.

Thirteen

❧

"Let me go," Chloe cried out. Panic swept over her body, forcing her to kick and fight against the arm pressing into her ribcage.

"Hey, you're bleeding. What's happened? Did you pass out again?" It was Philip.

She craned her neck, confirming it. He released her and studied her face. She couldn't help the tears that poured down her cheeks. She buried her face into his chest as she was overwhelmed with images of the children.

Gently pulling her away, he brushed her hair back as his worried gaze fell over her. "Stay still. You have a small laceration, but thankfully it won't require any stitches. Let me clean the wound and then I can—"

"We have to get out of here," she cried. A wave of nausea crashed in her stomach. "The children—they're—they're hurt."

He clasped her shoulders, inching her away from his torso. "Sweetie, what do you mean?"

She choked on a sob as mascara ran into her eyes. "There

are bones in there. Fucking bones in the walls." She closed her eyes, trying to force the awful images out of her mind. "Something terrible happened in there. These people—they..."

"Chloe," Philip sneered. "What did you do?"

She opened her eyes and shook her head. "Nothing! I-I don't know how to explain it. I was putting up the wallpaper, not knowing when you'd be back, and then I crashed through the wall—"

He cursed and turned away from her. Pacing in a line, Philip pressed his palms against his temples. Chloe watched as he walked in a staggered line, his eyes focused on the ground.

"Did you not hear me?" Chloe stepped in front of him, making him come to a halt. "There are fucking *bones* in there! We need to call the police."

"No!" Philip screamed.

She froze. Her blood went cold as Philip's jaw tightened. She hated the way anger painted his features, making his forehead throb and his nostrils flare. It seemed almost as if *he* had been cornered, caught red-handed.

He smoothed his shirt and cleared his throat. "My parents wouldn't approve of us calling the police. The Blackwells *never* call the police. We take matters into our own hands."

The image of the children on the floor flashed in her mind. She closed her eyes for a second, trying her best to make sense of why she'd been shown the grisly scene.

Then it clicked into place.

The faces of the people walking around and chanting were no longer blurry. They were crystal clear. And one of them stared right back at her.

"You," she whispered.

Philip's jaw relaxed. He reached a careful hand out toward her. "Chloe, I didn't—"

"It was you and your parents." The truth soured on her lips, but the pressure building inside of her released. Maybe she couldn't explain how she was able to have that memory, but now she knew the truth.

Now she understood why Philip had been so insistent about them doing the renovations. Now she realized the reason general contractors wouldn't accept jobs from the Blackwells.

They'd buried their secrets. In the walls.

But Chloe had come with a shovel, exposing their rotten secrets.

Philip's lip trembled. "I don't know what you think you saw."

Her face twisted and she took a step back. "You knew about those children, helped your parents..." But she couldn't finish the rest, couldn't relive the horrific memory. "How could you?"

Philip resumed pacing, raking his fingers through his hair. "I tried to help them. God knows I tried to help them."

Chloe remained silent as realization washed over his face. His family's secrets weren't theirs alone anymore.

Philip stopped pacing and sniffed. When he peeled his gaze upward, his bloodshot eyes met hers. "You weren't supposed to do any renovating without me."

Chloe placed her hands out in front of her, trying her best to create a barrier. She needed confirmation, some way to solidify that Philip was involved. Voices surfaced in her mind, their chanting hammering against her earlobes. "We forgive so that..."

"...we may be forgiven," Philip finished.

All the happy moments, the joyful memories of their relationship turned dark. He was a murderer.

"I'm not the only one who's killed someone though," Philip taunted.

Her ribs caved in. "What do you mean?"

"You know exactly what I mean," he sneered. "I know what you did."

Guilt pooled in her stomach. Chills ran down her arms as he approached her. Bending toward her, his hot breath met her earlobe. *Run, run, run.*

But she remained frozen in place. A deer in the head-lights, waiting for the impact.

"I know about Allen," Philip whispered in her ear. "And I know how you killed him."

No. She wanted to scream, explain how Harper was right, that it wasn't her fault, and that Allen taking his own life was not her fault.

"You don't know what you're talking about," she forced out.

Philip stepped away from her and motioned to the house. "I don't know what I'm talking about, hm? Oh, I knew Allen very well. You know how, Chloe?"

She eyed him, anger twisting every fiber of her being.

Philip stuck out his chest. "He was a member of our church."

Fourteen

⚬⚬⚬

er mind couldn't comprehend what he had said. She swallowed hard as she focused on the ground beneath her, tried to pull at anything tangible that might bring her back to reality. But his words haunted her.

"No," Chloe said shaking her head, "that's impossible. Allen was my—"

"Professor," Philip finished.

She looked up at him, trying her best to figure out how their worlds were connected. "I never told you that."

He shrugged as he approached her. "You didn't need to tell me. I've known Allen since I was in elementary school. He and his wife moved back to the mountains when he finished his teaching credentials. For someone who studied his work, you'd think you would've caught on earlier. His style was all over that place."

Her stomach churned. Here she was thinking that the property had called to her because of something she saw in it, but the reality was far more chilling. She'd connected with the building because Allen had left his mark on it with his design.

Chloe staggered, her knees buckling underneath her weight. Her head throbbed as thoughts carved into her skull. Philip was not who he said he was, but still he rushed to her side, placing his arms around her.

She couldn't help but weep.

"Shh," he tried to quiet her. "I know it's a lot to take in. But you must know that our family cared for Allen and his family. And if it wasn't for him, I wouldn't have met you."

Her heart pinched. She looked up at him. "What?"

He brushed a strand of her hair away from her eyes. "I was there at his memorial service and that's when I first saw you. I couldn't take my eyes off you. I knew you and I were supposed to be together. My family was crushed to learn of his passing, even more upset that he chose to take his life, but we know that God forgives. Which is why I was willing to forgive you."

She forced his arms off of her, pushing hard against his chest. "I didn't kill him!"

Philip nodded as he let out a chuckle. "No, you didn't *actually* kill him, but you can't say that you didn't push him to it. I mean, I understand the tether you can be. I don't fault Allen for being tempted by you."

Anger bloomed in Chloe's chest. "I-I didn't know he was married at first."

"We all make mistakes," Philip said, pointing to the house.

Her stomach twisted. "This is not the same. What you and your family did to those children..."

She couldn't take it anymore. Another flash of that

memory was enough to give her the strength to rise to her feet. "If you're not going to tell the police, I will."

Philip's jaw tightened. "You're not going to tell anyone. I forgave you for what you did to Allen. We forgive so that we may be forgiven."

Chloe looked to her left—their SUV. The keys would still be in the ignition. If she ran fast enough, she could beat him there.

She charged toward the driveway.

"Chloe!"

She ignored the way Philip's voice boomed. Picking up her pace, the SUV became her beacon of hope. She could drive into town and call for help there. A chilling thought washed over her.

What if the police already know about the Blackwells and chose to look the other way? What if all the officers used to be part of their cult too?

If not the police, she could at least call Harper. She just needed to run faster.

Her body slammed into the driver's side door, unable or unwilling to slow her pace. She clawed at the door handle, relief washing over her. She'd beat him to the vehicle.

But the door wouldn't open.

Panicked, she tried again, yanking at the handle to no avail. Frantic footsteps slowed behind her. The truth crushed her chest. The jingling of keys made her turn around.

"Looking for these?" Philip dangled the keys from his index finger.

She lunged forward. Her hand slipped, pulling his sleeve down. The two of them struggled against each other. Finally, Philip took a step back and swung his arm.

The car keys soared through the air, out of her reach, disappearing into the forest.

She looked at him in disbelief. Her only way to free herself from this man, and this property, was gone.

Philip wrapped his arm around her, turning her around until her back pressed against his chest. "You're not going anywhere. We're going to go back inside and wait for my parents to get here."

"Let me go!" she screamed. She twisted and struggled against his tight grip. Freeing one of her hands, she coiled her fingers into a fist and shoved her elbow down low behind her.

Philip let out a groan as he released his grip on her. Falling to his knees, he began retching through ragged breaths.

Chloe ran into the wilderness and didn't look back.

Pine needles clung to her pants as she moved through the thick forest debris. Ravens flew overhead as she weaved around the crowded trees. She didn't know where she was going, or whether this direction would lead to help.

But she needed to get away from Philip.

With his truth exposed, she couldn't help but think of what he would do to her. If he was capable of hurting children, what would he do to her?

She came to a clearing and cut to the right. The highway should be somewhere nearby. She could flag someone down and then get help that way.

A dark silhouette jumped out in front of her.

She came to a halt as she locked eyes with the ghostly woman in front of her.

"Chloe!" Philip screamed.

She swallowed hard, trapped between the two people trying to take her life.

The woman reached out and took Chloe by the throat.

Fifteen

You need to know.

A small feminine voice woke her. Chloe found herself on a wooden floor. Collecting herself, she patted the wound on her forehead, examining her fingertips for more blood. Had she fallen asleep? She looked around the old sanctuary. The pews were back in place, the original wallpaper riddled with handwritten text, and the bright sun peeked through the windows.

Then she heard a choir collectively singing the same melody.

Standing, Chloe walked toward the collection of voices. Fear grasped her heart. She recognized the song. Miss Bonnie had sung it just two days ago, trespassing in the main bedroom, but these voices sounded different—cheerful and childlike. Following the singing, Chloe twisted the doorknob to the side bedroom.

Only it was no longer a bedroom.

Children sat in a half circle on the carpeted floor, bobbing their heads to the piano music. The ghostly woman

—no, Callie—turned over her shoulder while she played, accompanying their voices. She was youthful, not a single mark on her, and had both hands intact.

"What are you doing here?" Chloe asked, stepping into the room.

They ignored her.

She reached for one of the children, but her hand went through their shoulder. She let out a soft cry as she stepped back. They all continued singing as if she wasn't there. Like she was the ghost.

Leaving the room, a bright light flashed before Chloe's eyes. She found herself transported to the back row of pews, next to the front door. She blinked; this was the old interior of the church building. Someone outside banged on the door, twisting the knob before she could get to it.

Callie strolled into the church, her arm encircled a man's. *Philip.* Chloe brought a hand to her mouth.

"Get away from her!" Chloe pushed Philip's chest.

But her body went through him.

No one could hear or see her. As if she didn't exist.

Chloe followed as the couple walked down the aisle of pews. They stopped before the altar. Callie released Philip's arm and spun around.

"I'm so proud of you," she said, smiling at him. "You've worked so hard to get that residency."

"I did it for us," Philip said, drawing her to him and planting a kiss on Callie's forehead.

A root of jealousy sprouted in Chloe's chest, but she forced herself to remember that she was being shown all of this for a reason. That he murdered three children and tried to dispose of their bodies, storing their bones in the walls of the church.

Philip circled his arm around Callie's shoulders. "I'm proud of you too. You've done so much for the children at school, and my parents are appreciative of how you have been leading Sunday school. It fits, right? The two of us. Pediatrician and elementary school teacher."

"I love you," Callie said.

Philip pulled her closer, embracing her. "Love you too."

Another flash erupted in Chloe's vision. She found herself outside of the church, but the day had transitioned to night. She looked down the driveway, eager to take its path and finally be free. She started toward the highway.

But she stopped.

"I can't," she whispered. "I need to know everything." Turning back around, the glow of light coming from the windows seemed almost inviting. *Almost.*

She raced toward the church, bounded up the porch steps, then paused. Something gnawed at her core; a warning screamed for her to flee. But she pushed open the doors instead.

Callie ran down the hallway. Chloe followed her to the closet on the left. Callie climbed inside, bumping into brooms and mops. Chloe slipped in beside her and waited.

A child cried out.

Callie leaned forward, pressing her weight against the wall to balance herself as she crouched. Chloe copied her movements, looking out the crack of the closet door.

Philip's mother rushed out of the Sunday school room.

"They're getting worse," she hissed.

Philip marched down the hallway, holding what appeared to be vials and bottles of liquid. "Mother, I–I don't know what to do. They should be getting better, not worse."

Philip's father followed behind him, shaking his head.

"You said you would be able to cure them. That's what you went to school for."

Philip held up a vial, examining it. He cursed and threw the bottle. It crashed against the wooden floor, liquid puddled. Callie covered her mouth, stifling a sob.

"We have to call it. Release them from their agony," Philip claimed.

His parents gave a worried look, but they both nodded.

Another flash stole Chloe away from the closet. She found herself reliving the awful nightmare she'd seen when she fell through the sanctuary wall. Philip and his parents, along with a man dressed in formal clergy clothes, circled the children's bodies on the floor.

Chloe no longer chose to stay quiet. Her footsteps echoed as she stomped down the rows of pews, screaming with fury as she charged into Philip.

But when she went through him, she found herself standing out in the field instead.

Frigid air cooled her skin. Philip hunched over a mound of dirt, out of breath, mud caked on his arms as he clenched a shovel.

"Now," Philip said to the night, "our secret is safe."

Chloe closed her eyes. *Philip, how could you? How could you do this?* She tried to force away the nightmare, force herself to believe it wasn't real. She choked on a sob as someone screamed her name.

She opened her eyes and found herself back in the woods surrounding the church standing in front of Callie's ghost. Philip cried out for Chloe again, his voice cracking on each syllable. Chloe dared to stare into the ghost's sad, sunken eyes. A chill ran down Chloe's back.

"You weren't trying to hurt me," Chloe whispered. "You were trying to warn me."

A soft smile lifted her ghostly lips. Callie loosened her grip around Chloe's neck. A warning. Yes, Callie had been trying to warn her about the monster she was engaged to. Chloe bit her lip as her gaze fell. She glanced at Callie's ashen skin, took in the jagged edges of torn flesh and bone.

All because of Philip's violence.

Guilt swirled in Chloe's stomach. Sure, she wasn't responsible for Philip's actions. But if Chloe never chose to come here to renovate the property, would Callie have been able to rest in peace? What about the children?

"I'm so sor—" Chloe's breath caught in her throat as she watched Callie's lower jaw fall open.

"You need to know," a voice called out.

Chloe's heart raced upon hearing those words. Not Callie's voice. Not Philip's.

The voice belonged to Allen.

Callie's mouth widened, exposing a dark void where her tongue should be. Fingertips inched beyond her lower teeth. Chloe winced as she attempted to move, but she was frozen in place.

She wanted to run, to escape the horror in front of her, but my god, why couldn't her legs move?

The familiar stench filled the space between them. The hand crawled past Callie's lips. The ghost released a guttural cry as the hand shot forward.

Chloe whimpered as the icy fingers clamped down on her neck. Its grip tightened, crushing against her windpipe. Chloe sucked in another tiny breath, swallowing the putrid air.

Her fate was sealed.

She was going to die.

But not without a fight.

Chloe clawed the decaying flesh as she stared at the limb coming out of Callie's mouth. Chloe cried out as she wiggled her thumb underneath one of the cold fingers squeezing her skin. Air returned to her lungs as its grip loosened.

She was not going to die. Not tonight.

Chloe screamed then gripped the hand and yanked hard. The forearm fell out of Callie's mouth, its bloody stump hitting the forest floor. Callie's ghost vanished.

Free. She was free.

"Chloeeeee!"

Her chest tightened. *Philiip.* She wasn't free after all.

Sixteen

~

Twigs smacked into Chloe's calves as she ran through the woods. Her head throbbed with every step, her body pleading with her to rest. But she had to make sure the truth was revealed. For the sake of the children and Callie.

They deserved better.

She hid behind one of the pine trees, trying her best to not let her presence be known. She peeked around the tree trunk; Philip was nowhere in sight. But he knew these woods all too well.

Her chest heaved as she contemplated. Screaming for help was useless among the expansive land. Her mind raced.

The road.

She could run down the long driveway to the main highway.

She stepped into the clearing, thick trees replaced by wild grasses and pine needles, the house in view. The front door slowly swung open, begging for her return.

Searing pain ignited across her scalp.

"Ahh!" she cried out.

By a handful of her hair, Chloe was yanked backward. Philip's hot breath against her cheek. "I didn't want to have to do this," he explained. "But you've given me no choice."

A harsh yelp left her lips as something cold and hard cracked her temple.

≈

PAIN RADIATED DOWN HER NECK. NAUSEA ROLLED her stomach like the reckless ocean tide. She dared to open her eyes, expecting Philip to have taken her back inside the house.

Instead, pine bark bit into her back as she looked around the dark woods.

Tight ropes bit into her skin as she tried to twist free from the tree trunk. Beyond the blooming light of a camping lantern, the silhouette of a man caught her attention. Philip was back to digging just as he had done in the vision Callie showed her.

Her stomach tightened. *Callie.*

She cleared her throat and tasted blood. Her head pounded, pleading with her to be quiet and not move. But she couldn't allow herself to become one of Philip's gruesome secrets.

"You killed those children," she spat out. "And you killed Callie for knowing."

Philip stopped digging. He slammed the shovel into the dirt and turned around. "You think you know the truth, but you don't. And if you don't quit squirming, I'll cut you limb by limb so you can't get away."

Her body stiffened. Blood ran down her throat as she swallowed hard, tears welling up in her eyes.

She was going to die.

Philip stalked toward her, then crouched. He cocked his head, and she could see tears in his eyes. "I wanted to be a doctor since I was young. I wanted to help people. So when I got older and a church member's son got sick, they begged my parents to let me try and figure out what was wrong. I examined that boy with the little medical knowledge I had, and you know what, I could see that he didn't have the classic presentation of gastroenteritis. Something about his case seemed different with his unremitting fevers and joint aches. Upon interviewing his parents, I discovered one of their cows was quarantined from the rest of the herd as it finished a course of antibiotics. Then it all made sense. He was drinking the infected cow's milk, strengthening my theory that he had a bacterial infection. I pleaded with the local pharmacist for the appropriate antibiotics to treat the boy for brucellosis. And I was *right*."

Questions circulated throughout her mind, but she kept quiet. She dug her thumbnail into the rope, testing its strength again. If she could just slip a hand free...

Philip brushed back his hair as he smiled. "The boy's parents were so appreciative. No lab work, no 'wait and watch,' and no need to rush him to an ungodly hospital in the city for a diagnosis. I was right! They knew I had saved their son right here in town. They said I had the healing hands given to me by God. After that, I knew that in order for me to save more children, I had to experiment, had to get some real-life experience. What better way than to help my community?"

Chloe swallowed the bile rising in her throat. Jamming

her nail down, her thumb wiggled free. The rope shifted as one of the lines went slack. She leaned forward, covering the loose part of her binding, and shifted her weight to free right arm.

Philip stood and paced. "I tried an experiment with some of the Sunday school children. I obtained a sample of the tainted milk to add the same bacteria to their Sunday school snacks, with a remedy ready for when they started showing early symptoms."

Chloe stilled. "But it didn't work, did it?"

Philip shook his head. "Three of them became too dehydrated with severe joint aches, even with me giving them around-the-clock care. My parents and grandfather insisted it must have been demons who had possessed them. After they passed, we knew we couldn't let the town know what happened. I didn't want it to end that way, I wanted to save them, but they didn't respond to the treatment."

Anger burned through Chloe. She couldn't make sense of his reasoning or how his parents could have gone along with this horrific plan. "So, you thought you were going to get away with it all?"

Philip started chuckling. "Was? Chloe, I *am* going to get away with it all."

The rope slipped and she broke away from its grip. She darted to the right as Philip lunged after her. A loud *crack* overhead stole their attention.

"Philip!" Chloe screamed.

A large tree branch crashed down. Philip cried out as he was slammed to the ground.

Seventeen

The wilderness was quiet. All Chloe heard were Philip's labored breaths. The huge tree branch pinned him to the ground. She could run, leave him to rot in the woods for what he'd done, and she'd finally be able to escape.

"Chloe," Philip wheezed underneath the tree's weight. "Please. I need you."

Her instinct pulled her close to him.

Kneeling, she met Philip's wild eyes. He winced in pain as the weight of the branch compressed his hips. He yelped, trying to push the log off of him.

"Hang on, Philip," Chloe said as she placed her hands on the wood. She was not a murderer. She couldn't leave him like this.

With all her might, she pushed against the weight, attempting to roll the branch enough that he could free his legs. The wood rocked against Philip's thighs, and he cried out in pain.

Throbbing pain radiated down Chloe's neck. Her vision blurred and her stomach swirled. She needed help. Her heart ripped apart, feeling stuck on this mountain. She looked over at the house and saw the mound of wet dirt piled next to the shovel. Her tears stopped. She looked at Philip crying out in pain as he tried to free himself.

He was going to kill her for exposing his secrets.

"Please," Philip said, panic tinging his plea. "You have to help me, Chloe."

She stood, hovering over him. He looked so helpless, so incapable of hurting another. He reached for her, begging for her help.

"Please," he murmured.

Chloe raked her teeth against her lower lip, unsure of what to do. She understood that Allen's death wasn't her fault, but this? If she were to walk away and leave him out here, could she live with herself?

"Fucking help me, Chloe," Philip commanded. "This is *your* fault."

"We forgive so that we may be forgiven, right?"

Philip's face twisted with disgust. "Don't fucking spout off that bullshit to me right now. Help me!"

She blinked and took a step forward. She wasn't a murderer. She would help him and let him live with the consequences.

The ground shook. The familiar foul aroma spread to her nostrils as wet soil parted. Decaying fingers clawed at the earth.

Chloe shrieked as she backed away. The same hand that had grabbed her now took hold of Philip's arm. He screamed out and thrashed, but the undead hand held on with an unshakeable grip. The ground rumbled and split open. Philip was pulled underneath, the arm tugging him to a shallow grave.

Philip clawed at the dirt pulling him below. "No!"

Soil filled his open mouth, stifling his agonizing screams. The tree branch splintered as it cracked in two, dragging dirt down into the gaping hole.

Philip was gone.

Chloe turned and ran toward the driveway. She gasped for air. The distance between her and the SUV shortened. Her hope for leaving this mountain, getting away from the ground that threatened to pull her down with Philip, came into sharper focus. Her body collided with the driver-side door. She yanked the car door open. Relief washed over her. She was going to get away from this god-forsaken place, return to the life she knew in the city. Hell, she'd crawl to her parents' home if needed.

But her heart sank. Her fingertips grazed the bare ignition. Tears flooded her eyes, blurring her vision as the crushing realization slammed into her.

Philip had thrown the keys into the forest. She was stuck. Alone.

She buried her face into her arms as panic laced through her. Bile clawed up her throat as she choked on sobs.

An icy hand pressed against her shoulder. Her chest tightened. *No.* She couldn't be pulled into the ground like Philip. She didn't deserve the same fate.

Three sets of eyes stared back at her.

The youngest girl dug her hand into the pocket of her dress. The other girl and boy stood behind, not saying a word. The little girl held out her right hand to Chloe. Peeling back her small fingers, metal glinted in the moonlight.

Chloe's fear evaporated, and she forced herself to accept what lay in the girl's palm.

The keys to the SUV.

"Go," the girl said. "Before she gets you too."

Chloe gently plucked the keys from the girl's hand. The cool metal restored her hope. Chloe turned and looked through the passenger window. She gazed at the open field before turning back to face the children.

"They can't hurt you anymore," Chloe whispered.

The three children shared a look. Their fingers laced together as they held hands. The slightest bit of a smile brightened each of their faces. Chloe shut the car door and jammed the keys into the ignition. The engine roared to life. She rolled down the window, ready to say thank you.

The children were gone.

Chloe fastened her seatbelt and adjusted the rearview mirror. Relief washed over her when she didn't see anyone coming after her. She put the car in reverse, carefully navigating as she turned around in the driveway. Gravel spewed into the air as she peeled out of the driveway.

Once on the road, she calmed her breathing as best she could. Her wide eyes scanned the road. She was going to get away. She was safe.

A blur of brown shot out in front of her vehicle. She shrieked. Turning the wheel, the car whipped across the road. The steering wheel shook underneath her tight grip. She slammed on the brakes. Sweat collected against her hairline. Her heartbeat pounded against her ears. She could hear the faint sounds of a deer bounding into the forest.

"Fuck this mountain," she sneered.

Tracing the steering wheel, she steadied her grip and blew out a breath. Chloe stepped on the gas and continued down the road. Cool air blasted across her skin from the open window as she increased her speed.

Now, she was headed home.

Eighteen

TWO MONTHS LATER

The hot summer sun shone down on the crowd gathered in the cemetery. Rows of chairs lined the grass, reaching almost as far back as the parking lot. Solemn greetings mixed with sobs as people found their way to their seats. Chloe tucked in her newly dyed red hair to conceal her identity into the black sunhat and covered her eyes with large black sunglasses.

The local high school band played instrumental music, notifying attendees that the ceremony was about to begin. Chloe accepted the cardstock program from a young girl and found a seat in the back row. She smoothed her black skirt and looked over the cover of the pamphlet. Pictures of the deceased children solidified what she knew had happened to them. Their school portraits, full of smiles and groomed hair, displayed the sorrowful fact that they had died too soon.

All because a sadistic man thought he'd made a medical breakthrough, thought he was some kind of god.

Chloe opened the pamphlet and sucked in a breath. A portrait of Callie stared back at her. The caption below

Callie's name described her unfathomable love and adoration for keeping children safe.

The tap of the microphone stole her attention.

"Good afternoon, everyone," a man with combed-over hair greeted the crowd. He adjusted his waistband over his thick belly. "Today, we mourn collectively. We honor our community members who were taken from us too soon. I have lifted my own prayers of thanksgiving to the anonymous individual or individuals who notified the authorities of the remains discovered at the Blackwell property. I know we all have questions, many that I do not know the answers to, so we will allow local authorities to continue their investigation. Instead, we remember and uplift those precious souls who are no longer with us."

Chloe leaned back in her chair. Sweat collected at the back of her neck. She tucked a loose strand of hair back into her hat as the man's voice droned. *Today is about them,* she reminded herself. A sense of pride swelled in her heart. *At least they now had peace.*

Two elderly women shuffled in the row in front of her, obstructing her view of the stage. The women leaned into each other, whispering back and forth.

"No sign of Philip yet," one said, her floral print dress a little garish among the other funeral garb.

"Probably ran off with that fiancé of his. I can't believe the Blackwells are in custody. I'm telling you, someone has set them up. They're good people. It's a shame Philip decided to live in the city. Now his parents are suffering a false accusation alone," the one on the right said, fanning herself with the program.

Chloe's stomach twisted with irritation. She wanted to correct them, tell them that Philip's fiancé was the one who had told the police everything. Instead, she remained quiet.

She was there to honor Philip's victims, not make a scene.

At the close of the service, the speaker, later identified as the mayor of Hallowed Pines, motioned to the crowd to join him in the covered picnic area for a barbeque banquet. Chloe waited until most of the people had rushed toward the buffet line before she rose from her seat. She tucked the program into her purse and made her way to the statue that was close to where the mayor stood.

The steel plaque listed each of their names: Tristan Anderson, Amelia Larsen, Brittany Bishop, and Callie Tucker.

The metal warmed her palm. Chloe whispered her condolences, emphasizing how sorry she was for what they'd had to endure. Though nothing she could say would change their outcome, she hoped they at least would be allowed to rest in peace.

"Oh darling," a voice said behind her.

Chloe retrieved her hand, straightened and turned to see who was behind her. Miss Bonnie smiled and took a step forward.

"It's so nice to see you, Chloe," Miss Bonnie said, lifting her arms to embrace her.

Chloe stepped back. "Oh, no. You've got the wrong person."

Miss Bonnie adjusted her glasses as she cocked her head. "Oh, my apologies. You look like someone I know."

Chloe scratched underneath her hat, allowing a chunk of red hair to hang freely. "That's okay. I must be going now. Have a good day."

She side-stepped the elderly woman, thankful Miss Bonnie didn't come chasing after her. Chloe was ready to get as far away from this small town as possible. She belonged in the city.

As she walked to her silver sedan, a dark silhouette appeared out of the corner of her eye. Chloe whipped around, feeling the pressure of someone watching her. She glanced at the crowd gathered around folding tables, plates piled high with food, smiles replacing sorrowful looks.

Chloe slipped into her car, unsure about who might have been watching her. She drove out of the parking lot and back toward the city, without daring to check the rearview mirror.

Nineteen

R ain hit the city streets, heightening the scent of smog and sewage. Chloe rushed past groups of people, making her way to the golden lights illuminating the restaurant's logo. She hated being late.

Opening the glass door, she was greeted by a girl with a buzzcut and nose ring. "Welcome to Parkside. Do you have a reservation?"

Chloe shrugged off her black raincoat, folding it on her forearm. "It should be under Harper Renson. I'm running a little late, so she might already be here."

"Oh, yes," the hostess said, tapping the tablet mounted to the hostess stand. "Right this way."

Chloe weaved around tables of people feasting on delicious meals and conversations. The place was packed for a Wednesday evening, but the excitement of being amongst so many people was exhilarating. *This* was her home.

Harper hopped out of her seat and embraced her. "Oh my god, look at you!"

Chloe smoothed her red bob, curling the ends under her chin. "Thanks, I got it done last week."

The two of them sat and ordered cocktails from the happy hour menu. Glancing over the menu, Chloe's mouth watered. Not a single mention of peanut butter and jelly sandwiches. She'd sworn off them for the rest of her life, not wanting to taste a single memory tied to the Blackwell property.

"How have you been?" Harper asked, setting her menu aside.

Chloe folded hers and sat up straighter. "Good, I guess. It's been a little hard finding a place close to the city, hence why I was running late."

"And your parents? They still well?"

Chloe shrugged as she took a sip of her iced lemon water. "They're fine. Same as always which is why I need to get the hell out of there."

"Chloe," Harper whined. "I already told you that you could come and stay with me and Jazmyn. Seriously, we would love to have you. Our cats would love to have another person scratching their ears too."

Chloe leaned back as the waitress set down their cocktails. She waited until it was just the two of them, then took a sip and relished the flavor of the lemon liquor spreading across her tongue. She licked the sugar-rimmed glass and shook her head. "No, this time I want to try being on my own. I think it's what I need."

Harper reached across the table and took Chloe's hand. "Fuck, are you okay?" She looked around the crowded restaurant, dropping her voice down low. "Have you heard from—"

"No," Chloe cut her off. The image of Philip sinking into the earth, pulled down by Callie's grasp flashed in her mind. "And I won't."

Harper patted Chloe's hand before picking up her drink. "Good. So, I have some news I wanted to share."

Chloe's eyes lit up. "As do I, but yours first."

Harper let out a breath as she pulled her phone out of the breast pocket of her vest. Tapping the screen, she faced the phone toward Chloe. "I'm going to ask Jasmyn to marry me."

Chloe scooped up the phone, marveling at the picture of the engagement ring Harper had selected. "Oh my god, congratulations!"

"I'm really nervous, to be honest. Have any advice?" Harper took back her phone, tucking it back into her pocket.

Chloe stiffened. She thought about how Allen had promised to start a new life with her. Then how Philip had gotten down on one knee. She had come so close to a happy ending, yet here she was alone for the first time in years.

"Just stay true to who you are," Chloe explained. "And make sure Jasmyn isn't a fucking murderer first."

Harper laughed uncomfortably. "Of course. Oh, and your news?"

Chloe plucked a business card from her purse. An electric feeling took over her, making her buzz with excitement. "I'm starting a new chapter in life. And hey, even my parents approve of this more 'lucrative' career move."

"What, no designing anymore?"

"After what happened with my last *project...*" Chloe slid the card across the table, waiting in anticipation for her best friend's reaction. "I think this will better suit me."

Harper took the card in hand. Her dark eyebrows shot up as she beamed with excitement. "Holy shit. You'll make an excellent realtor."

Epilogue

She swept dead leaves off the stoop, away from the front door. Yet, the increasing wind yanked them from the trees, littering the steep driveway. The gray sky warned of rain, even though the temperature was warm. Such was the unpredictability of autumn in the Bay Area.

Chloe opened the front door and placed the broom into the side closet. Cool mist wisped from the diffuser, blasting vanilla and sandalwood scents to mask the fresh paint. She pulled out her cell phone to check the time. They'd be there any minute.

Stepping into the only bathroom, Chloe tucked her hair behind her ears, then rehearsed the property details in the mirror. "This house was built in the 1950s, rich with Bay Area history. It is believed that an ancestor of Marilyn Monroe lived here, even entertaining some of her friends during the summer of '55."

She blew out her breath. Sure, she didn't go into detail about how mold had to be eradicated last month, or how the old tenants left this place in complete shambles. But if she could make this sale, her life would change forever.

She dreamed of being able to afford her own place in the city, a place to call her own and hers alone. Completing her first sale as a real estate agent would bring her one step closer to her new dream.

A knock on the front door boomed through the hall.

"Hello?"

Chloe walked out of the bathroom and plastered on a warm smile. "Hi! You must be Mr. Reese. I'm Chloe Atchinson. It's nice to finally meet you in person instead of talking over Zoom. How was the flight from Houston?"

He shook her hand and cleared his throat. "Delayed due to thunderstorms, but I finally made it."

Chloe smoothed a loose thread on her sleeve, tucking it behind her button cuff. "Oh, and Mrs. Reese? Isn't she going to be joining us as well? It'd be great to finally meet her."

Pulling out his phone, he tapped on the screen. "My wife just texted me to say she's running a little late, but she'll be here any minute. Please, start showing me around."

Chloe began the tour. She pointed out the three bedrooms, though only two were permitted by the city. However, she made sure to mention that the far bedroom might be best suited for a home office, complete with a city view. Once they made their way toward the kitchen, the man sighed and leaned against the counter.

"Huh, no dishwasher." He *tsked*. "My wife isn't going to like that."

Chloe bristled but remained calm. "I'm sure that could be easily added. I can pass along my contractor's information if you'd like. He's a solid, dependable handyman."

Mr. Reese shrugged. "Maybe."

As they continued the tour, Chloe led him to the back patio. He groaned as he paced the perimeter of the fence. "Seemed much larger in the photos," he scoffed.

Chloe fiddled with her hands, tucking them into the pockets of her jumpsuit. "Oh, I forgot to show you the electric fireplace. It creates an amazing ambience."

The two of them shuffled back inside. Chloe could tell he was losing interest. She just needed to convince him this place was perfect for them. After all, it checked off all their boxes— a decent fixer-upper with rich history.

The front door opened. A petite woman slipped inside, peeling off her peacoat. "Sorry I'm late," the woman called.

"Hi, honey," Mr. Reese said, greeting his wife with a kiss. "This is Chloe Atchinson."

Chloe blinked twice, trying her best to wake from what was surely a nightmare.

But she couldn't deny the person standing in front of her.

"Callie," she whispered.

"Hi, Chloe. It's nice to meet you," the woman said sweetly.

It couldn't be. Callie was dead, the one who pulled Philip to his own grave. Yet this woman looked just like Callie's picture from the memorial, not the ghost who'd haunted her at the Blackwell property.

"I'm not so sure this is what we want," Mr. Reese explained, "but let me go take another look at the yard again."

Chloe watched the man walk down the hallway toward the sliding glass door. When he was out of sight, she fixed her gaze on Callie. The woman's cold stare froze her blood.

"You're dead," Chloe muttered.

Callie cocked her head. "Funny because I've never felt more alive."

"I saw it," Chloe said through a shaky breath. "You – you pulled Philip down and—"

"Sent him where he belongs," Callie finished. "Next thing I know, I'm the one alive in the wild grass on the Blackwell property. I even watched you drive away that night."

Chloe ran her teeth over her trembling lower lip. "But why? Why are you here now? What have I done to you?"

"You should have left when you had the chance," Callie said, twisting the end of her hair. "I tried to reach out to you – to warn you – yet you were so fixated on staying to profit off that horrible property. And Allen?"

Chloe's eyebrows lifted at the name.

Callie shook her head. "You really thought you could bury your secrets? You're really no better than Philip. I should have pulled both of you down to your deaths."

Darkness overtook the room. Not even the sunlight poured through the windows. Goosebumps spread across Chloe's skin. She twisted in place, attempting to run.

But she was frozen in place.

"Please," Chloe whimpered. "Don't do this."

Fingers curled around her shoulder. Chloe screamed as she grabbed the hand.

"Hey!"

Chloe blinked. Light and colors flooded her vision. She stared up at Mr. Reese holding his palms out in front of him.

"When were you going to let us know there's an electrical issue?" He scoffed as he looked past Chloe. "Sweetie, are you sure you want to buy this?"

"Well, you know what they say..."

Chloe whipped around. She staggered back, gripping the kitchen counter. She was wrong. So wrong. Callie wasn't only seeking revenge on Philip. Now she was after *her*.

She smoothed her dark hair over her shoulder. "A house can be a home if it has such good bones."

Preview the next book in
A HORDE OF DEAD POETS
collection!

AVAILABLE NOW

One

"Thou shalt not fall into the hellfire of temptation, Maidens, if one never forgets to remain vigilant and always, always beware the goblins' trickery," the vicar said, his voice booming through the church. "Their evil fruit, once tasted, is never forgotten."

Kitty only half listened to the sermon while her gaze drifted to the young man in the pew before her. The back of his neck looked smooth like silk, one small freckle at its center, begging to be kissed. He brushed a lock of curly auburn hair behind his ear with fingers as perfect as any master sculptor could fashion. Kitty blushed at her own thoughts, turning to her Bible. She had fancied Duncan for as long as she'd known him, yet his eyes always drifted toward her sister, Esther. As neighboring children they'd played with stray dogs in the village lanes and made mud pies near the glen on rainy afternoons. Those days seemed long ago now that she was eighteen.

A leg bumped into Kitty, startling her, and she met her sister's hard stare. Kitty rolled her eyes and straightened in her seat, pretending to be captivated by the sermon just as her mother and aunt were doing beside her.

The vicar continued his warning against the demonic goblins, a theme he'd warmed to ever since one of the local women withered away after eating the creatures' wicked fruit. *Foolish woman.* Kitty never understood how one could be warned from the time of early childhood about ignoring the goblins' call and yet still decide to eat the fruit anyway. Perhaps the woman hadn't wanted to live any longer or had been too tempted to discover the fruit's taste.

Only two women had ever survived the goblins and lived to tell their tale: Kitty's mother, Laura, and Aunt Lizzie. She glanced at her mother out of the corner of her eye, wondering what she'd looked like as her body lay withering and aged, her starving form nearly bones. If it hadn't been for the bravery of Aunt Lizzie, her mother would've been sacrificed to the Goblin King, her soul trapped in his realm for eternity.

"And that is the conclusion of today's sermon," the vicar said, his gaze meeting Kitty's as though he knew she hadn't paid him her full attention.

"Come on, girls," their mother said, clinging onto her Bible. "Let's have a picnic for lunch, shall we?"

Aunt Lizzie brushed her hands down the front of her dress. "That sounds delightful, Laura." But something in her eyes remained empty, just as they had been ever since her husband died in the war, alongside Kitty and Esther's father. And it was only a year ago that Aunt Lizzie's son had grown ill, his tiny body wracked with fever until he passed away. At some point another streak of gray had been added to her beautiful blonde curls.

Duncan turned around and gave a bashful grin to Esther.

"We have a batch of new apples. They'd be perfect for your pies if you want to come by the market tomorrow?"

Esther smiled politely, but only said, "Sure, I'll send Kitty."

"See you then, Kitty." Duncan's expression never wavered, but the spark of hope vanished from his eyes.

As they left the church, warm sunlight broke through the clouds. A flock of pigeons called to each other as they flew past. The day was perfect for a picnic as the four of them walked home along the winding trail to their meager cottages. Aunt Lizzie's home was on their property, but both cottages were in need of work. Even with the number of pies their bakery sold, there never seemed to be spare coin to spend for repairs. Thankfully Duncan had been willing to lend a hand, when he wasn't working at the market or tending the fields of his parents' home.

The chickens squawked and pecked at their feed in front of the cottage, and Kitty sat beside Esther on the stairs as her sister read a letter she'd received from her friend Winifred, who'd married and moved away to London the prior year.

"Duncan will notice you one day." She bumped her shoulder into Kitty's. "I promise."

"If you fall for him, I won't mind. You deserve happiness." It was half a lie, but Kitty did want to see her sister's dreams come true. If only her own could come true as well...

They ate cucumber sandwiches and sausage rolls, while laughing about the neighbor's pig getting loose and other bits of minor town gossip, until it was time for Aunt Lizzie to go home.

Aunt Lizzie gave the sisters each a hug goodbye, then

became serious, as she always did before departing, her words so familiar to Kitty they had become a bore.

"I strengthened the wards on the windows," she said, "so make certain to say your prayers after kissing your iron crosses before you sleep." The goblins were said to fear iron the most.

"We never forget." Esther nodded.

"Of course we will," Kitty added. Women didn't vanish that often, and even though Kitty knew goblins would of course never come to them, she repeated her prayers every night if not for herself, then at least for her aunt and mother's comfort.

That night, Kitty lay in bed, peering up at the ceiling. "Protect us from evil. Protect the women in our village from those who would harm them. Draw us close to your heart, Lord, that we may not fall into the temptation of evil. Save those who have fallen by the hands of goblins before us— may their souls rest in eternal peace forever."

ENJOY THESE NOVELLAS IN ANY ORDER!

A HORDE OF DEAD POETS

BETTER GRAVE THAN THIS — JESSICA CRANBERRY

SOME RAIN MUST FALL — MEG DAILEY

SUCH GOOD BONES — LENN WOOLSTON

IN THE HAUNTS OF GOBLIN MEN — CANDACE ROBINSON S.G.D. SINGH

DEATH'S MAIDEN — ELLE BEAUMONT

DESCENDANTS OF THE BIG HOUSE — A. GONZALE LEWIS

A HORDE OF DEAD POETS

Acknowledgments

They say it "takes a village" to raise a child, but the same is true for writing a book. I am grateful for my writing tribe with whom this story would have never come into the world. As such, I want to take a moment to offer my gratitude to the following people who helped bring this story to life.

To Carla, Jess, and the entire Percy's Heart Press, thank you for inviting me and my work to be part of this stellar collection. Your vision, insight, and encouragement have made this story stronger; I am forever grateful for you taking a chance on me.

To my fellow A Horde of Dead Poets authors, it is an honor to sit next to you on the bookshelves. I appreciate your excitement for this series, your wonderful stories, and your support in getting my novella out into the world.

To my loving family and friends, you know how long I've been dreaming of this day when I can write an acknowledgment in my own published work. Thank you for your continued love and support as I continue to pursue this crazy thing called being an author.

To Kim, Holly, Megan, and the rest of my writing tribe, thank you for always supporting me. I could not endure the highs and lows of the publishing journey without you. Your friendship through all of this is something I will always cherish.

To Jared, the love of my life and more, thank you for encouraging me in all moments. Thank you for helping me through every step of life and for always being open to reading my stories. I love you more and more each day.

Finally, thank you, dear reader, for spending time with my dark tale. I genuinely hope you enjoyed it, and I cannot thank you enough for picking up this story.

About Lenn Woolston

Lenn Woolston is a horror and dark fantasy author. Previous literary work includes "Hungry," a YA horror short story in the Far from Home anthology, published by Off Limits Press. She continues to craft stories that always take a walk on the darker side. After all, strange is her cup of tea.

www.lennwoolston.com

instagram.com/lennwoolston

threads.net/lennwoolston

youtube.com/lennwoolston

Also by Lenn Woolston

Hungry

www.ingramcontent.com/pod-product-compliance
Lightning Source LLC
Chambersburg PA
CBHW050416110726
47899CB00008B/2740